THOMAS CRANMER

FROM THE PICTURE BY GERBIC IN THE NATIONAL PORTRAIT GALLERY
FROM A PHOTOGRAPH BY MESSRS. WALKER AND BOUTALL

THOMAS CRANMER

BY

ARTHUR JAMES MASON, D.D.

LADY MARGARET'S READER IN DIVINITY AND FELLOW OF JESUS COLLEGE
CAMBRIDGE, CANON OF CANTERBURY

METHUEN & CO.
36 ESSEX STREET W.C.
LONDON
1898

TO THE BEVEBEND AND LEABNED
THE MASTER AND FELLOWS OF JESUS COLLEGE
I OFFER
THIS SLIGHT ACKNOWLEDGMENT OF THE EXTEEME KINDNESS
WITH WHICH THEY HAVE WELCOMED ME INTO THE SOCIETY
OF WHICH CKANMER WAS TWICE FELLOW

PREFACE

THIS book is not intended to be an exhaustive account of the great Archbishop's life, or to go minutely into every question that may be raised in connexion with it. It is rather an attempt to use in a fairly broad fashion the results of the researches of many students, with a view to setting Cranmer as a living and intelligible figure before the English reader of to-day. He is still, as the late Lord Houghton called him in the preface to his Recantacyons," the most mysterious personage of the British Reformation ;" but the history of the sixteenth century is gradually becoming known, and Archbishop Cranmer has received a large share of sympathetic study.

The materials for his biography are, first, his own letters and writings. These have been collected and published during this century by Mr. H. Jenkyns, and also by the Parker Society. I have generally used Mr. Jenkyns' collection. Next in value are the two documents printed in the Camden Society's Narratives of the Reformation —both of them first-class authorities. Ralph Morice's notes—the more important document of the two—were written for Archbishop Parker, and are the work of Cranmer's principal secretary, a man of intelligence and resource. It may be that they are

occasionally coloured by partiality, but it is to the credit of Archbishop Cranmer that he should have been able to inspire such devoted loyalty into the heart of his servant. Foxe's Acts and Monuments stand in a secondary position. His account of Cranmer is largely drawn from the two documents just mentioned. He frequently, especially in reporting conversations, endeavours to improve upon his original, which detracts from the historical value of his work; otherwise its vivacity and picturesque force make it delightful reading. The works of Burnet and Strype are most useful to the student, especially in the pieces justificatives contained in their appendices ; but both authors require constant verification. Among later works Todd's and Hook's lives are, in their respective ways, serviceable, though neither of them succeeds in presenting a satisfactory portrait of Cranmer.

For an account of the special documents relating to the Archbishop's last days, I would refer the reader to the fourth volume of Mr. R. W. Dixon's noble History. I have to thank Mr. Dixon for having lent me his copy of the remarkable tract called Bishop Cranmer's Recantacyons, which, as he justly says, he was the first to use. But I have even more to thank him for his History itself. My own book is little else than a putting together of various parts of that work in which Cranmer is spoken of. I trust that it will not be thought disrespectful if I observe that Mr. Dixon's treatment of Archbishop Cranmer becomes more and more appreciative in the successive volumes. No doubt that is partly because, like other good men, Cranmer himself became worthier of his regard; but I believe that it is partly also because the more deeply Cranmer's

character and career are studied, the more attractive they make themselves felt to be. Among historical figures, as among those of actual life, the fewest mistakes are made by him, who, while exercising a just criticism, exercises it with a charitable resolve to put the best construction which facts will allow upon actions and motives. Mr. Dixon has taught us to do this with men as widely apart as Gardiner and Latimer, as Bonner and Hooper. If my pages may help

Englishmen to do likewise with a greater person, I shall indeed be thankful.

Canterbury, Holy Cross Den, 1897.

Since writing the above, I must add my best thanks to Mr. James Gairdner for having most kindly presented me with a copy of Bishop Cranmer's Eecantacyons, of which he was the Editor.

CONTENTS

CHAP.		PAGE
I.	CRANMER'S LIFE UNTIL THE DIVORCE	1
II.	CRANMER AND PUBLIC AFFAIRS UNDER HENRY	44
III.	CRANMER AND THE REFORMATION UNDER HENRY	81
IV.	CRANMER UNDER EDWARD VI.	119
V.	CRANMER'S LAST YEARS	165

Thomas Cranmer (2 July 1489 – 21 March 1556) was a leader of the English Reformation and Archbishop of Canterbury during the reigns of Henry VIII, Edward VI and, for a short time, Mary I. He helped build the case for the annulment of Henry's marriage to Catherine of Aragon, which was one of the causes of the separation of the English Church from union with the Holy See. Along with Thomas Cromwell, he supported the principle of Royal Supremacy, in which the king was considered sovereign over the Church within his realm.

During Cranmer's tenure as Archbishop of Canterbury, he was responsible for establishing the first doctrinal and liturgical structures of the reformed Church of England. Under Henry's rule, Cranmer did not make many radical changes in the Church, due to power struggles between religious conservatives and reformers. However, he succeeded in publishing the first officially authorised vernacular service, the Exhortation and Litany.

When Edward came to the throne, Cranmer was able to promote major reforms. He wrote and compiled the first two editions of the Book of Common Prayer, a complete liturgy for the English Church. With the assistance of several Continental reformers to whom he gave refuge, he changed doctrine in areas such as the Eucharist, clerical celibacy, the role of images in places of worship, and the veneration of saints. Cranmer promulgated the new doctrines through the Prayer Book, the Homilies and other publications.

After the accession of the Roman Catholic Mary I, Cranmer was put on trial for treason and heresy. Imprisoned for over two years and under pressure from Church authorities, he made several recantations and apparently reconciled himself with the Roman Catholic Church. However, on the day of his execution, he withdrew his recantations, to die a heretic to Roman Catholics and a martyr for the principles of the English Reformation. Cranmer's death was immortalised in Foxe's Book of Martyrs and his legacy lives on within the Church of England through the Book of Common Prayer and the Thirty-Nine Articles, an Anglican statement of faith derived from his work.

Arthur James Mason DD (4 May 1851 – 24 April 1928) was an English clergyman, theologian and classical scholar. He was Lady Margaret's Professor of Divinity, Master of Pembroke College, Cambridge, and Vice-Chancellor of the University of Cambridge.

Early life:

The third son of George William Mason JP, of Morton Hall, Retford, Nottinghamshire, by his marriage to Marianne Atherton Mitford (born 1821 in India), a daughter of Captain Joseph George Mitford (1791–1875), of the Madras Army, Mason was educated at Repton School and Trinity College, Cambridge. The third of four sons, his youngest brother, Charles Evelyn Mason, was killed in the Zulu War of 1879. His brother William Henry Mason was a High Sheriff of Nottinghamshire. His sister, Harriet, was a poor law inspector and another sister, Agnes founded a religious community. Their grandfather, J. G. Mitford, was the son of Bertram Mitford (1748–1800) of Mitford Castle in Northumberland.

Career:

Mason was elected a Fellow of Trinity College in 1873 and was a college tutor from 1874 to 1877, when he went to Cornwall as Canon of Truro. His departure from Cambridge was at the urging of his friend Edward White Benson, who had been appointed as Bishop of Truro and wanted Mason to act as diocesan missioner.

In 1884, after Benson had been translated to Canterbury, Mason took up a benefice as Vicar of All Hallows-by-the-Tower, Barking, in the City of London, where he remained until 1895. That year he returned to Cambridge as Lady Margaret's Professor of Divinity (1895–1903) and also became a Canon of Canterbury Cathedral. He was a Fellow of Jesus from 1896 to 1903, before serving as Master of Pembroke from 1903 to 1912. In 1908 he was elected Vice-Chancellor of the University, continuing in the post for two years.

As well as works on theology and biography, Mason wrote and translated hymns. As "A. J. M.", he was a contributor to the Dictionary of National Biography.

Private life:

On 11 January 1899, Mason married Mary Margaret, a daughter of the Rev. G. J. Blore DD, Honorary Canon of Canterbury Cathedral and a former Head Master of King's School, Canterbury. They had two sons, Paul and Lancelot, and a daughter, Mildred. Paul became a diplomat and was ambassador to the Netherlands in the 1950s, while Lancelot followed his father into the Church and was Archdeacon of Chichester from 1946 to 1973.

Arthur James Mason died at Canterbury on 24 April 1928.

THOMAS CRANMER

CHAPTER I

CRANMER'S LIFE UNTIL THE DIVORCE

THE subject of this biography has, perhaps, received more indiscriminate praise and more indiscriminate censure than any other ecclesiastic of the English Church. His predecessor Thomas Becket, and his successor William Laud, both martyred like himself, alone rival him in this respect. Cranrner was a man not free from infirmities, and it is no object of the following pages to make light of them; but it must be taken into consideration that the circumstances in which he lived were difficult beyond parallel in English history; and no one—at any rate no one who values the principles of Reformed Catholicism—can withhold, when he is acquainted with the facts, a thankful admiration for the man who, by the providence of God, steered the Church of England so well through the first perils of the Reformation.

Cranmer's family is said to have been of Norman extraction. A Norman gentleman bearing the same name and the same arms was attached to one of the French embassies in Henry VIII.'s time, and was

entertained at Lambeth by the Archbishop. Their original seat in England was in Lincolnshire, where, at the end of the sixteenth century there was still " an ancient mansion-house of antiquity, called Cranmer Hall," with the arms of Cranmer still to be seen in t|ie windows. 1 The great-grandfather of the Archbishop, by marriage with an heiress, came into the property of Aslockton, in the adjoining county of Nottingham.

Aslockton lies in the pleasant and fertile Vale of Belvoir, between Nottingham and Grantham, on the banks of the little river Smyte. On a piece of firm ground, amidst the morasses through which the stream once wandered, rises a bold grassy mound, the only survivor out of three which are said to have once existed there. The mounds were formerly known as the Bailey Hills, and are no doubt the remains of some ancient fortification; but the villagers call the one which remains " Cranmer's Mound," and the tradition is that the Archbishop, whether in youth or in later life, used to sit upon this mound and listen to " the tuneable bells" of the neighbouring church of Whatton. Accounts differ as to the site of the house where the Cranrners lived; but there on July 2, 1489, was born the future Archbishop, the second son of Thomas and Agnes Cranmer, the sixth in a family of seven, having two brothers and four sisters. 2

Cranmer's youth was not altogether happily spent.

1 Morice p. 238. The arms were originally three cranes, but Henry VIII. changed them

into three pelicans in their piety, as a sign of Cranmer's readiness to shed his blood for his children in the faith ; " for you are like to be tested," he said prophetically, "if you stand to your tackling."— (Ibid. 251.)

2 Some part of his father's estate seems to have come into the hands of the Archbishop, although his elder brother lived and had

His father <(did set him to school with a marvellous severe and cruel schoolmaster." According to one account this schoolmaster was " a rude parish clerk." [1] Cranmer afterwards complained that he " appalled, dulled, arid daunted the tender and fine wits of his scholars," and said " that, for his part, he lost much of that benefit of memory and audacity in his youth that by nature was given unto him, which he could never recover." [2]

Not all his " audacity," however, was taken from him. His father, though always " very desirous to have him learned, yet would he not that he should be ignorant in civil and gentlemanlike exercises; insomuch that he used him to shoot, and many times permitted him to hunt and hawk, and to exercise and to ride rough horses." These pursuits were maintained in mature life. When he was Archbishop of Canterbury, according to his secretary's account, " he feared not to ride the roughest horse that came into his stable, which he would do very comely; as otherwise at all times there was none that would become his horse better. And when time served for recreation after study, he would both hawk and hunt, the game being prepared for him beforehand, and would sometime shoot in the long-bow, but many times kill his deer with the crossbow; and yet his sight was not perfect, for he was purblind." [3]

The father did not live to see the results of his training of the boy. He died when Thomas was twelve years old,

a numerous family. In a State paper of 1529, " Mr. Dr. Cranmer " is named as one of those who have corn to dispose of in the parish of Aslockton.

[1] Narratives of the Reformation p. 218.
[2] Morice p. 239. [3] Ibid. p. 240.

and was buried in Whatton Church, where a dignified and uncommon-looking stone covers his grave, incised with his effigy, in the costume of a gentleman of Henry VII.'s reign. The widowed mother sent Thomas, at the age of fourteen years, to Jesus College at Cambridge, which had been founded seven years before. His college tutor was not a man to be of much help to an inquiring youth. " The scholar of such an one I was," he writes, " who when he came to any hard chapter, which he well understood not, would find some pretty toy to shift it off, and to skip over to another chapter, of which he could better skill." [1] There " he was nozzled," says a contemporary, " in the grossest kind of sophistry, logic, philosophy, moral and natural (riot in the text of the old philosophers, but chiefly in the dark riddles of Duns and other subtile questionists), to his age of twenty-two years. After that, he gave himself to Faber, Erasmus, good Latin authors, four or five years together, unto the time that Luther began to write; and then he, considering what great controversy was in matters of religion (not only in trifles, but in the chiefest articles of our salvation), bent himself to try out the truth herein: and forasmuch as he perceived that he could not judge indifferently in so weighty matters without the knowledge of the Holy Scriptures (before he were infected with any man's opinions or errors), he applied his whole study three years to the said Scriptures. After this he gave his mind to good writers, both new and old, not rashly running over them, for he was a slow reader, but a diligent marker of whatsoever he read ; for he seldom read without pen in hand, and whatsoever [1] Jenkyns iii. 472.

made either for the one part or the other, of things being in controversy, he wrote it out if it were short, or at the least noted the author and the place, that he might find it and write it out by leisure; which was a great help to him in debating of matters ever after. This kind of study he used till he were made Doctor of Divinity, which was about the thirty-fourth of his age."

It is interesting to observe that the date at which this evidently well-informed writer speaks of Cranmer's turning from scholasticism to the study of Erasmus and other good Latin authors, was the date (1511) at which Erasmus himself began to lecture in Cambridge as the Lady Margaret's Reader in Divinity. Erasmus, in a well-known letter of the year 1516, contrasts the barren scholastic studies, which were all that Cambridge had had to offer a few years before, with the knowledge of literature and of the Bible which had recently been developed there. 2 The approximate date at which Cranmer is said to have devoted himself to the study of Scripture (1516) is the date of the publication of Erasmus' Greek New Testament.

There can be no doubt that the young Cranmer was personally influenced by the teaching of Erasmus, although there is no record of direct intercourse between the two men at Cambridge. Later on, after Warham's death, the great man of letters, writing to deplore the loss of his chief patron, expresses his thankfulness that Providence has made some compensation for him, " inasmuch as the deceased Archbishop's place and dignity has been taken by Thomas Cranmer,

1 Narratives of Reformation p. 219.
2 Erasmus Ep. cxlviii. ; cf. Mullinger Univ. of Camb. vol. i. p. 515.

G THOMAS CRANMER

a professed theologian, and a most upright man of spotless life, who, without my asking him, has promised that he will not be behind his predecessor in his care and kindness towards me; and what he freely promised, he has equally freely begun to perform, so that I may feel that Warham has not been taken away from me, but is born again in Cranmer." 1

It is, perhaps, not much to be wondered at, that there was no more intimate friendship between him and Erasmus at the University. Cranmer was twenty-one years junior to Erasmus; and he was always of a retiring temper. It was not likely that he would thrust himself forward in academic circles, any more than elsewhere. It cannot be concluded from the silence of Erasmus that Cranmer was no great scholar in those days. He was commonly appointed to examine candidates for degrees in divinity at Cambridge, and distinguished himself by insisting upon the knowledge of Scripture. 2 His reputation for learning was so well established in the University, that about 1524, upon the recommendation of Capon, Master of Jesus, he was invited by Cardinal Wolsey, along with a few other rising Cambridge scholars, to accept a canonry in the new Cardinal College at Oxford, an honour which Cranmer declined. 3

Cranmer does not appear at first to have had the intention of entering Holy Orders. Soon after gaining his fellowship at Jesus, in 1510 or 1511, when he was one or two and twenty, " it chanced him," in the quaint language of Ralph Morice, " to marry a wife." Who

1 Erasmus Epist. mcclxi.
2 Cooper's Athena Cantabr. i. 146 (after Foxe).

and what his wife was is not certain. Foxe says that she was " a gentleman's daughter," and that Cranmer " placed the said wife in an inn, called the ' Dolphin/ in Cambridge, the wife of the house being of affinity unto her/'j 1 That a gentleman's daughter, in those days, should be related to the wife of a respectable innkeeper was not impossible; bat Foxe's account of the matter seems to be not wholly correct, for it would appear from the report of Cranmer's last trial that she was living at the "Dolphin" before her marriage, and was not only "placed" there afterwards. It " was objected that he, ... being yet free, and before he entered into Holy Orders, married one Joan, surnamed Black, or Brown, dwelling at the sign of the Dolphin in Cambridge. Whereunto he answered, that whether she was called black or brown he knew not; but that he married there one Joan, that he granted." 2

It was evidently not an exalted marriage; but scholars in those days were often content with homely alliances, and there is not the smallest reason for supposing that there was anything clandestine or otherwise wrong about it. Cranmer's fellowship at Jesus was vacated by his marriage; and to support himself he " became the common reader at Buckingham College," 3 now Magdalene. But within a year his wife died, in childbirth; and it is a proof of the esteem in which he was held among those who knew him best, that his own college re-elected him fellow. He was ordained soon after, for in 1520 he was appointed one of the

1 Foxe viii. 4 (I quote from the eel. of 1843-9).

2 Jenkyns iv. p. 100. The "Dolphin," according to Mullinger's Univ. of Camb. i. 612, stood " at the Bridge Street end of All Saints' Passage." Part of Trinity occupies the site.

3 Morice p. 240.

University preachers, and graduated the year after in divinity. A lecturership in that science had been established at Jesus, and Cranrner held it. 1

It is pleasant to observe that Cranmer's friendliness towards his College continued after his promotion to Canterbury. In June, 1533, he sent the Master a buck, "to be bestowed amonges your company within your College. And," he adds pleasantly, "forasmuch as you have more store of money, and also less need than I at this season, therefore I bequeath a noble of your purse towards the baking and seasoning of him. And whensoever I have so much money beforehand as I am now behindhand, I shall repay you your noble again." 2 Two years later he interposed somewhat peremptorily to preserve the College from a troublesome inquiry with which Cromwell threatened it, most heartily requiring Cromwell to suspend his judgment, and to repel all manner of information and suit in the case, until he heard further from the Archbishop. 3

A most bitter enemy describing those Cambridge years says of Cranmer, that by means of an agreeable though not particularly brilliant nature, and by immense, if ill-spent, industry, he obtained the distinction of being made a Doctor, 4 and so laid the foundation of subsequent honours. " He had in his favour," says the same writer, " a dignified presence, adorned with a semblance of goodness, a considerable reputation for learning, and manners so courteous, kindly, and pleasant, that he seemed like an old friend to those whom he encountered for the first time. He gave signs of modesty,

1 Morice, p. 240. 2 Jenkyns i. 34.

3 Ibid. i. 133.

4 It was in 1526, according to Cooper Ath. Cantab, i. 146.

seriousness, and application." 1 Cranmer probably expected and desired to spend all his days in the quiet round of academic duties, or perhaps to settle eventually in a country benefice. But one of those accidents which alter the history of the world, brought him suddenly into public life.

In order to understand the nature of that accident, it is necessary to state briefly the position of affairs with regard to the so-called Divorce of Henry VIII. and Catherine of Aragon. To give this transaction the name of a divorce is really to prejudge the question. Divorce, in the strict sense of the term, is unknown to Christianity. Man and wife, according to the Gospel laws, can never be anything else to each other but man and wife; and if Henry and Catherine had ever been truly man and wife, no act of Church or State could legitimately set either of them free in the lifetime of the other to marry another person. But it is a matter of grave and reasonable doubt whether Henry and Catherine were ever truly man and wife. Catherine had been at an earlier time the wife of Henry's elder brother Arthur, the Prince of Wales. According to Catherine's own statement, which there is no need to doubt, her marriage to Arthur had never been more than a legal and nominal marriage. But nevertheless it was sufficient to form an obstacle to marrying Henry. Catherine had been publicly married to Arthur, first by proxy and then in person. For the few remaining months of the young Prince's life the two had lived together in the eyes of the world as man and wife. To propose, therefore, after Arthur's death, as was done

1 Bishop Cranmer's Recantacyons p. 3. Regarding this work see Dixon iv. 490.

by Henry VII., and urged by Ferdinand the Catholic, that his widow should be transferred to his brother, was to outrage every Christian sentiment. Only a low and unworthy conception of the marriage tie could have made it possible to entertain the proposal. There were many at the time of Henry VIII.'s marriage, among whom was Warham, Archbishop of Canterbury, who questioned whether it was possible for such an union to be allowed. But unhappily the Papal system of dispensations had already accustomed men's minds to seeing the laws of marriage tampered with. Martin V., in 1418, had permitted John, Count of Foix, to marry his deceased wife's sister. [1] When Catherine's own confessor objected to the proposed marriage with Henry, her father could silence the objection by pointing to Emmanuel, King of Portugal, who was living happily with the sister of his first wife, by dispensation from Alexander VI. [2] The conscience of Europe had been still further paralysed by seeing permission given by the same wicked Pope to Ferdinand II., King of Italy, to marry his own aunt— a precedent many times followed by later popes, down to the present one, who allowed the late Duke of Aosta, propter nimiam pietatem, to marry his sister's daughter. But Alexander VI. himself refused consent to Catherine's marriage with Henry; and so did Pius III. It was the next Pope, Julius II., a man of little higher character than Alexander, who first gave a dispensation for a man to marry his brother's widow; and he did so—the point is much to be observed—not on the ground that, after examination, Catherine's marriage

1 Thomassin. Vet. et Nov. Eccl. Discip. part II., lib. iii. cap. 28 sect. 10. See Mr. Knight Watson's letter in the Guardian, Dec. 13, 1882.

2 Hook's Warham p. 195.

with Arthur proved to have never been a real one. He expressly sanctioned the union whether it had been real or not. Had Julius II. been content to deviate no further from the law of God than Alexander had done before him, England might have remained subject to the Papacy. It was Julius II. who lost the English Church to Rome, by professing to make valid, in any case, a marriage which nothing could justify.

That Henry VIII. was prompted by high and sacred considerations to seek release from his union with Catherine would be a paradoxical thesis to maintain. He was tired of her. As early as 1524 he had ceased to treat her as a wife. [1] Another affection began to occupy all his mind. The way in which the matter of the divorce was conducted turned what might have been a right and Christian transaction into a tyrannous and cowardly oppression of a helpless lady. When it was found that Catherine could not be brought in private to adopt Henry's view of the situation, then every artifice was employed to prevent her from offering effectual opposition. Cardinal Wolsey (who did not wish for the divorce, but who found that his position, if not his life, depended upon carrying it through) set himself to prejudice the Queen in the judgment of her best advisers. While Catherine was made to treat the subject as a religious secret, and was debarred from communicating with Spain or Rome, the King's party were pressing busily forward. With the greatest stealth, lest the Queen should hear of it, embassies on the subject were sent backwards and forwards to the Pope and to the French King. Catherine was looked upon as an adversary to be alternately brow-beaten and outwitted ; 1 Brewer Reign of Henry VIII. ii. 164.

and the King, so far from putting on the appearance of a man under a burden of conscience from which he sought relief, was living a life of extravagant gaiety, with Ann Boleyn ostentatiously thrust forward as if she were already Queen.

If only Rome could have adopted a firm attitude at this juncture, although it was too late to retrieve the mistake of Julius, yet England might at least have been lost with dignity. But the poor bastard who held the see of Rome was incapable of taking a firm attitude of principle. Clement VII. at one moment assented to the institution of a collusive suit before Wolsey as legate, in which, without Catherine's knowledge, Henry was summoned to answer on a charge of living with his brother's wife. 1 At another moment he promised to give Henry a dispensation to marry a new wife without deciding for or against the validity of his first marriage. 2 These were the weapons of unscrupulous weakness. At length, a commission was issued to Wolsey and Campeggio to sit as joint commissioners for the hearing of the case; but the duplicity of Clement provided Campeggio with instructions on no account to allow the case to come to a decision ; and after many months of obstruction, it was finally revoked, in July 1529, to Rome. Things were thus brought to a standstill.

The King's disgust at this conclusion of the work of the legates drove him " for a day or twain " from London to Waltham Abbey. He was attended by two heads of Cambridge houses— Edward Foxe, Provost of King's, as almoner, and Stephen Gardiner, Master of Trinity Hall, as secretary. These were the two men who had lately managed the King's matter. It was by their 1 Brewer ii. 187. 2 Ibid. ii. 228J 230.

exertions that Clement VII. had been induced to issue his commission for the trial. The " harbingers" happened to quarter them at Waltham in the house of a gentleman named Cressy. There they met Dr. Cranmer. An outbreak of the plague had driven him from Cambridge, where two of Mr. Cressy's sons were pupils of his; their mother also being akin to him. The three men were " of old acquaintance, and meeting together the first night at supper had familiar talk concerning the estate of the University of Cambridge, and so, entering into farther communication, they debated among themselves that great and weighty cause of the King's divorcement." Cranmer modestly said that he had " nothing at all studied for the verity of this cause," nor was " beaten therein," as Gardiner and Foxe were; " howbeit, I do think," he said, " that you go not the next way to work as to bring the matter to a perfect conclusion and end. . . This is most certain, that there is but one truth in it, which no man ought or better can discuss than the divines." It had already been recommended that the Universities should be consulted— indeed Cranmer himself had been put on a commission to represent Cambridge in the matter. 1 But Cranmer not only advised that the opinion of the learned men of the kingdom should be sought; he advised that the King should then proceed to act upon it without waiting for the " frustratory delays " of the ecclesiastical courts. When the Divine law had been set forth, " then his Highness, in conscience quieted, may determine with himself that which shall seem good before God, and let these tumultuary processes give place unto a certain truth." 2

1 Narratives p. 219. 2 Morice p. 241.

" If the King," so ran another version of what Cranmer said, " rightly understood his own office, neither Pope, nor any other potentate whatsoever, neither in causes civil nor ecclesiastical, hath anything to do with him. or any of his actions, within his own realm and dominion ; but he himself, under God, hath the supreme government of this land in all causes whatsoever." l

Even this advice of Cranmer's had no great novelty about it, for Gardiner himself had a year before threatened the Pope face to face, at Orvieto, that if he did not give sentence as required, England would go over to the opinion that a Pope was as unnecessary as he was useless.² There were already many men of that opinion in England, although it was not much avowed. But Cranmer's utterance came exactly at the right moment for the King. When Foxe and Gardiner reported to him their interview with Cranmer, " Mary," said the King, " I will surely speak with him, and therefore let him be sent for out of hand. I perceive that that man hath the sow by the right ear." ³

Cranmer probably never expected his words to be brought to the King's knowledge ; and Foxe, the martyrologist, is most likely right when he affirms that he earnestly entreated to be left to his peaceful privacy. If Gardiner could have foreseen the future, he would certainly have done all in his power to give effect

1 Baily's Life of Fisher p. 89. The words form no part of the valuable document (published by Van Ortroy in 1893) which served as the chief basis of " Baily's " work ; but they are likely enough in themselves.

2 Brewer ii. 252.

3 Foxe viii. 7. Wordsworth Eccl. Biog. iii. 130 quotes the story from Baily's Life of Fisher p. 90 in the form, " The King swore, by his wonted oath, Mother of God, that man hath the right sow by the ear."

to that desire. But things were otherwise ordered. Cranmer came to the King at Greenwich. Henry professed to take him into his confidence. He told him that he never " fancied woman better " than Catherine, and that he only sought for a dissolution of his marriage because it was a burden to his conscience. " Therefore, Mr. Doctor," he said, " I pray you, and nevertheless, because you are a subject, I charge and command you (all your other business and affairs set apart) to take some pains to see this my cause furthered according to your device, as much as it may lie in you, so that I may shortly understand whereunto I may trust." 1 Henry had a way of making men believe him; and Cranmer, the most guileless and unsuspicious of men, was not slow to be persuaded. He undertook the task, and threw himself heart and soul into it.

The first duty assigned to him was to cast his opinions on the subject into the form of a treatise. At the King's request he was received, while writing it, into the house of the Earl of Wiltshire, the father of Ann Boleyn. It has been alleged that Cranmer had been for a long time past a chaplain and friend of the family. 2 The conjecture is based upon a misunderstanding. There is no evidence whatever that Cranmer was acquainted with the Boleyns before this date; but he now formed a warm and zealous attachment to them —especially to Ann—and his interest in writing for

1 This is Foxe's account, viii. 8.

2 See Mr. Gairdner's note in Brewer ii. 223. I do not know on what grounds Mr. Gairdner admits that Cranmer was ever a chaplain of Wiltshire's. On the other hand it would appear that Cranmer was already acquainted with Cromwell, and had occasionally acted on his behalf : Calendar of State Papers of Henry VIII. iv. 4872.

the divorce became keener as he learned to desire the King's marriage with his host's daughter.

As soon as the book was written it was used to influence the opinion of the Cambridge doctors. Cranmer had, it seems, already disputed on the subject there, and by his skill in argument had converted to the King's side five or six of those who had been the leading champions of the opposite view. It is probable that he now repaired again for a time to Cambridge in furtherance of the cause. 1 His book, at any rate, was widely circulated there, and with effect. It is satisfactory, however, to note that he was not personally implicated in the discreditable intrigues by which Gardiner and Foxe obtained a majority for the King in the

Cambridge Senate-house. By the time that the University gave its decision Cranmer was far away, discussing the matter with more eminent personages than the Cambridge scholars. 2

Towards the end of 1529 a new embassy was despatched to the Court of Rome. At the head of it, by a strange and audacious selection, was the Earl of Wiltshire, Ann Boleyn's father. Cranmer was a member of this embassy, along with Stokesley, Bishop-Elect of London, and others. They found the Pope at Bologna, where the Emperor—Queen Catherine's nephew—also was; and Cranmer probably witnessed there Charles's long-deferred coronation at Clement's hands. 3 The

1 The occurrence to which Morice refers (p. 242) is evidently the same as that mentioned by the anonymous biographer (p. 220), who places it before the writing of the book. Both, however, speak of his visiting Cambridge afterwards.

2 See the account of the Cambridge proceedings in Mullinger i. 618, where the date is given ae 1529 instead of 1530.

3 February 24, 1530.

Emperor's presence, no doubt, made the prospects of the mission less hopeful, and Wiltshire failed to obtain the Pope's consent to have the cause settled by the Archbishop of Canterbury. When the Emperor's back was turned Clement " more than three times told " the Bishop of Tarbes " in secret, that he would be glad if the marriage " between Henry and Ann " were already made, either by a dispensation of the English legate or otherwise, provided it were not by his (Clement's) authority, or in diminution of his power as to dispensations and definition of Divine law." 1 Clement had no high-minded determination to see right done by Catherine; but he would not endanger his own position, nor give mortal offence to the Emperor. Wiltshire returned to England a few days after Charles had left Bologna, but Cranmer stayed behind, and moved with the Pope to Rome. There he went on busily with his negotiations, alternately sanguine and dejected. On July 12 he wrote from Rome to a fellow-agent at Bologna (it is the earliest letter of his of which anything is preserved)—

"As for our successes here, they be very little; nor dare we to attempt to know any man's mind, because of the Pope; nor is he content with what you have done; and he says, no friars shall discuss his power. And as for any favour in this Court, I look for none, but to have the Pope with all his cardinals against us." 2

A little later, the prospect appears to him somewhat less gloomy—

" As concerning the brief, the Pope never granted us

1 Le Grand Histoire du Divorce iii. 400.

2 Quoted in a letter from Croke to the King (State Papers of Henry VIII. iv. 6531), which is in part printed by Burnet Reformation i. 155.

none after our device, whatsoever Sir Gregory (Cassalis) hath written. Mary, this he did—he willed us to devise a brief; and if it liked him, he would ensign it. But when it was devised, faults were found in it, and it was given to the Cardinal Sanctorum Quattuor to amend; but he amended it after such fashion that it was clean marred for our purpose. Since that time we have had so many new devised and changed again; yea, and moreover, when the Pope hath granted some of our devise, the Emperor's oratory hath made such exclamations against the Pope that all hath been changed. I never knew such inconstancy in my life. And to shew you plainly my thought, I suppose we shall never have none according to our mind, so long as the Cardinal Sanctorum Quattuor, our utter adversary, beareth this authority. Notwithstanding, the Pope is contented, and I trust we shall have shortly one brief metely good after mine opinion, but not with such terms as we would have it." 1

Personally, the Pope seems to have made a not unfavourable impression upon Cranmer, to judge from later sayings of his. Clement's manners were amiable, and he sought to do Cranmer a pleasure. He appointed him to the office of " Penitentiary "—according to some, for Henry VIII.'s dominions, according to others, for the whole Papal communion itself. 2 Whether this was the lucrative position which some have considered it, or not, the conferring of it was a high compliment. But in spite of compliments, Cranmer returned, as Morice says, "not answered with the Bishop of Rome." He arrived in England in September, 1530, to find that things

1 State Papers of Henry VIII. iv. 6543. a See Wordsworth Ecd. Biogr. iii. 135.

were past the diplomatic stage, and that preparations were making for independent action.

In December 1530, the King, under the guidance of the ruthless Cromwell, struck his first blow at the papal power by laying the entire clergy of England under a Praemunire, for having accepted Wolsey as legate of tlie Pope, although it had been at Henry's own instance that he was made legate. The Convocation, which met at the beginning of the new year, thought it best to make no resistance to this tyrannical measure, but to purchase the King's forgiveness by a large vote of money. Before, however, their gift was accepted, it was determined by the King and his advisers that the Church should be forced to acknowledge explicitly its subjection to the Crown. Into the deed which conveyed their grant of money they were required to insert, among other expressions, a clause which acknowledged the King as " alone Protector and Supreme Head of the Church, as of the clergy, of England." The clause was long and vigorously debated in Convocation. Messages went backwards and forwards between the clergy and the King. The King was ready to modify his language by admitting the words "after God" into the title of " Supreme Head." Even so the clergy would not agree to the title. At last, on February 11, Archbishop Warham proposed an amended recognition of the King as " sole protector, only and Supreme Lord, and, as far as the law of Christ allows, Supreme Head also " of the English Church and clergy. The amended form was received in silence. When the Archbishop reminded the assembly that silence must be taken for consent, a voice replied, "Then are we all silent." The Convocation of York

followed the example of Canterbury, although some of the bishops of the northern province thought fit to publish protestations, explaining the sense in which they admitted the title; to which protestations the King himself replied in a conciliatory manner, declaring that he intended no intrusion into the proper functions of the episcopate.

It is to be observed that in all the debates upon the new title—at any rate in this stage of proceedings—no one thought of suggesting that the King was encroaching upon the rights of the Pope. Later on, indeed, it was supposed that by this act the King was substituted for the Pope as Supreme Head of the Church of England; and, as a matter of fact, if the title was to mean anything at all, it involved a repudiation, or restriction, of powers which the Papacy had been permitted to exercise in England. But the designation of " Supreme Head," or "sole Protector," or "only and Supreme Lord" of the English Church, had never been used or thought of in connexion with the Bishop of Rome; and in arrogating it to himself Henry VIII. made no reference to the claims of the Papacy; nor did those who opposed the designation oppose it in the interests of the Papacy: they opposed it in the interests of the liberty of the English Church, and in the interests of the spiritual authority assigned by Christ to the apostolic ministry. When (mistakenly or not) they were satisfied that Henry was only claiming what his predecessors had always claimed, and had no designs upon the internal constitution of the English Church, the anti-papal drift of the King's new style woke no perceptible alarm. The nation, both in Church and in State, was well accustomed to anti-papal enactments, and there were few who objected to them so strongly as to think it worth while to speak out. The voice which emphasised the silence of the Convocation of Canterbury, when the new title was read out, expressed the feelings of the English Church" and nation.

But the next year, 1532, saw the Supreme Head beginning to interfere with the liberties of the English Church in a new way. In answer to a supplication of the House of Commons, and in spite of temperate and earnest expostulations on the part of the hierarchy, the King forced upon Convocation the memorable Submission of the Clergy. By this they bound themselves not to put forth any new canons or ordinances without the King's assent, and agreed that the existing canons should be examined by a committee of the King's appointment, with a view to annulling those which might be found prejudicial to the realm, or onerous to the laity, retaining in force the remainder if they should receive the royal authority. The King is said to have exclaimed, in the midst of these transactions, that owing to the oaths of canonical obedience to Rome taken by the bishops at their consecration, the English clergy were but half his subjects. But so far were the English clergy from objecting to the new regulations for fear of causing a breach in the connexion with Rome, that the Convocation in this same year presented a petition (which bore fruit in an Act of Parliament) for the abolition of the Annates, or first-fruits, which the bishops had been accustomed to pay to the Roman treasury. The clergy urged, in this petition, that if the Pope should offer opposition, then, " forasmuch as all good Christian men be more bound to obey God than any man, and forasmuch as St. Paul willeth us to

withdraw ourselves from all such as walk inordinately," it should be ordained that " the obedience of the King and his people be withdrawn from the see of Rome,"— for which they alleged the precedent of Charles VI. of France and Benedict XIII. The Act of Parliament which gave effect to this desire of the clergy was not at once made known. It was the King's wish to make one more effort to bring Clement VII. round to his matrimonial projects, and only when that effort failed was the royal assent formally given to the Act. 1

In these discussions and determinations Thomas Cranmer had had no share, that we know of, although he appears to have been in England and about the person of the King in the first half of the year which saw the Supreme Headship acknowledged by the clergy. 2 In January of that year, although he did not start till later, he was appointed to the difficult post of ambassador to the Emperor, Charles V., with a special view to the question of the marriage. He had recently been made Archdeacon of Taunton. 3 Two of his despatches from Germany to Henry VIII. are extant, and reveal in him considerable sagacity and power of observation. 4 He was still engaged in the cause of the King's divorce among the German princes and divines, though with no conspicuous success, when he was recalled to England, and to the true work of his life.

On August 23, 1532, the liberal-minded Archbishop

1 See Dixon i. 113, 136, foil.

2 Todd i. 29. Jenkyns i. 1.

3 But see Calendar of State Papers of Henry VIII. iv. p. 2698, according to which Gardiner held the office at this time. Morice (p. 243) speaks of Cranmer's promotion as that of " the deanery of Tanton in Devonshere," which is manifestly inaccurate.

4 Jenkyns i. 6—16.

Warham, the patron of Erasmus, died. It was under him that the clergy accepted the Supreme Headship and made their submission. It was under him that they had petitioned for separation from Rome, in case the Pope should insist upon the payment of Annates. But Warham was still Legate of the Apostolic See, and before he died he wrote a protest against the consequences which might flow from the measures in which he had taken part, to the derogation of the rights of Rome, or of the prerogatives and liberties of the Church of Canterbury. It was too late, however, to protest, and Warham's successor was destined to see, and to help on, the logical results of what had been done under Warham.

Most writers treat it as a strange and astonishing thing that the King should have selected Thomas Cranmer to succeed to the vacant primacy, as if he had been an unknown man. Doubtless there were other men who had occupied a more conspicuous position in the eyes of the English Church, but there is no evidence to show that Cranmer's own contemporaries were surprised. An important foreign embassy was the usual step to ecclesiastical promotion. Tunstall, Stokesley, and Bonner successively passed from such embassies to the great see of London; Gardiner to that of Winchester; Lee to that of York. It was not altogether surprising that one who had been entrusted with missions so important as those which Cranmer had of late discharged, should be put into the see of Canterbury. True, his career up to the year 1529 had been that of a quiet student of the University, but it was not without point that Cranmer himself, when forced, a few years after, to take notice of a foolish slander against his

earlier life, replied—"If you had but common reason in your heads, you that have named me an ostler, you might well know that the King, having in hand one of the hardest questions that was moved out of the Scriptures these many years, would not send an ostler unto the Bishop of Rome, and to the Emperor's council, and other princes, to answer and dispute in that so hard a question." 1 Undoubtedly all open-eyed men must have expected to see Cranmer soon promoted to some high ecclesiastical position, and there is probably some grain of truth in the tale which the Papist Harpsfield relates in a distorted form, that Archbishop Warham, in conversation with his nephew, had predicted, not without distress, that Cranmer would be appointed to succeed him. 2

Beyond all question, the person who was most surprised and least pleased by the appointment was Cranmer himself. He cared nothing for honours and dignities, and was probably only anxious to have done with his embassy and to retire into private life again. There was the more reason for his doing so, inasmuch as in the course of his wanderings amongst the learned men in Germany, " it was his chance " again 3 " to marry a kinswoman of one of theirs," Margaret, the niece of the well-known Osiander. Such careless statements are made about matters of this kind, that it may be worth while to point out how widely Cranmer's marriage differed from that, for instance, of Martin Luther. Martin Luther was a friar; his wife a nun. Both of them had believed themselves called by a special

1 Morice p. 271.
2 Pretended Divorce of Henry VIII. (Camclen Society) p. 178.
3 Morice p. 243.

vocation of God to the life of virginity, and had solemnly vowed that they would never change that estate. Cranmer had done nothing of the sort. The canons of the Western Church, indeed, at the time of his ordination forbade the marriage of the clergy, but he had never taken any vow of celibacy. And now the entire authority of the canons was shaken in England by the submission of the clergy. Cranmer held himself in conscience free. No doubt his residence in Germany, where the marriage of the clergy had long been an accepted thing among liberal-minded men, inclined him the more to a step which he was well assured that the laws of God and of the primitive Church allowed. He had, it appears, already sent his wife into England when the tidings of his great appointment reached him, and the difficulties which his marriage would cause must have added much to the reluctance with which he accepted the charge laid upon him.

That reluctance was unfeigned. " There was never man came more unwillingly to a bishoprick, "he said at his last trial, " than I did to that. Insomuch that when King Henry did send for me in post that I should come over, I prolonged my journey by seven weeks at the least, thinking that he would be forgetful of me in the meantime." It was a cruel and unjust retort that was made: " The King took you to be a man of good conscience, who could not find within all his realm any man that would set forth his strange attempts, but was enforced to send for you in post to come out of Germany." 1 No doubt it was with a view to subserving the purpose of his divorce, that King Henry had 1 Jenkyns iv. 92.

nominated Cranmer for Archbishop. When he thanked the King for his promotion, Henry is reported to have told him that he ought rather to thank Ann. 1 But by the time that Cranmer was fully in his new seat, the Convocation of Canterbury, by a large majority, following the lead of the Universities, had pronounced the marriage of Arthur and Catherine to have been a full marriage, and that the Pope had no power to dispense in such a case. 2 Not to speak of the second order of the clergy, probably half the bishops in England—certainly Gardiner, Stokesley, Longland, Standish, Veysey—would have vied with each other to pronounce the divorce. The Act forbidding all appeals to Rome had just been passed by Parliament, and those bishops knew what they were about; None of them evinced any hesitation in taking the King's side, whatever the Pope might say or do. But the King chose a man of larger capacity than any of them to do his work, and Cranmer moved slowly into his place.

Cranmer was consecrated in St. Stephen's Chapel at Westminster on March 30, 1533, by Longlaud, Bishop of Lincoln, Veysey, Bishop of Exeter, and Standish, Bishop of St. Asaph. A curious point was raised at his consecration owing to the anomalous circumstances of the moment. Hitherto, for some centuries, all English bishops had taken an oath of obedience to the Pope, and then another to the King, which was intended to deprive the former of political significance. Cranmer had, in the natural course of things, received the usual bulls from Rome for his consecration. He proceeded, according to precedent, to take the usual oaths. But

1 Bishop Oranmer's Recantacyons p. 4.
2 April 5, 1533.
UNTIL THE DIVORCE . 27

Henry VIII., as has been said already, had lately been exercised in mind with regard to these oaths; and it seemed necessary to be more than ordinarily careful lest the new Archbishop should find himself, like Wolsey, involved in a Praemunire. Accordingly, Cranmer prefaced his oath to the Pope by a protestation, before a notary and witnesses, that he held it to be more a form than a reality, and that he did not intend by it to bind himself to anything contrary to the law of God, or against the King and commonwealth of England, and the laws of the same; and that he reserved to himself liberty to speak and consult of all things pertaining to the reformation of the Christian religion, and the government of the English Church. 1 A great deal has been made of this action of the Archbishop's, both at the close of his own life and since. " He made a protestation one day," cried Martin at his last trial, " to keep never a whit of that which he would swear the next day." Cranmer's answer was characteristic. " That which I did," he said, " I did by the best learned men's advice I could get at that time." 2 It was his weakness to endeavour to shift the responsibility for his actions upon others. There would have been some force in the rejoinder, that all the learning in the world could not rid him of a perjury, if indeed Cranmer had had clearly in view, at the time when he took his oath, all that he was led to do afterwards. But at the time, he probably meant little less by his oath to the Pope than most bishops of his age and country did. A

1 The oaths are given in Jenkyns iv. 247, foil. When Dixon i. 158, note f, says that

Cranmer made certain omissions and insertions in the usual form, he seems to be confounding the form of oath before consecration with that before receiving the pall, also given by Jenkyns. 2 Jenkyns iv. 21.

Langton or a Chichele might as justly be charged with perjury as Cranmer.

It ought to be clearly understood that Cranmer, at the time of his accession to the throne of Warham, was not the Cranmer of the middle of Edward VI.'s reign— still less was he the modern Protestant he is often taken for. Though he had most likely been on the side of practical reform from the epoch of Erasmus' sojourn in Cambridge, and was always open-minded, even upon doctrinal subjects, yet when he was made Archbishop his opinions were those of most of the scholars of the day. It is true that the one subject on which he seems to have already made up his mind most definitely, in a reforming direction, was that of the Papal usurpation and its practical consequences. When, three years afterwards, he preached upon this subject at Canterbury, " I said," he writes to Henry, " that these many years I had daily prayed unto God that I might see the power of Rome destroyed; and that I thanked God that I had now seen it in this realm. And I declared the cause wherefore I so prayed. For I said that I perceived the see of Rome work so many things contrary to God's honour and the wealth of this realm, and I saw no hope of amendment so long as that see reigned over us; and for this cause only I had prayed unto God continually, that we might be separated from that see."!

It may appear surprising that a man of such sentiments could take any oath of obedience at all to the see from which he daily prayed to be separated. But one or two facts deserve to be taken into consideration before judgment is passed, even if they are not held sufficient 1 Jenkyns i. 170.

to justify Cranmer's action. No one, of course, in those days was expected to believe the Pope to be infallible; and no thoughtful contemporary of the Borgias, Roveres, and Medicis could imagine that in practice the Roman Curia was always right. An oath of canonical obedience to the Pope could not possibly bind a man to blind subserviency. Every prelate who had taken part in the Councils of Pisa, Constance, and Basel, had sworn the same kind of oaths; yet they did not feel themselves thereby precluded from criticising the authority to which they swore, or even from combining to depose a Pope who gave scandal. Archbishop Cranmer desired by his protestation to vindicate for himself the same liberty. He had, as yet, no doctrinal quarrel with the Popes, and no wish permanently to break off ecclesiastical communion with them. But he felt deeply that they were guilty of grave errors in working —especially with regard to the marriage law—and of pernicious usurpations in government. Despairing of their correction by milder measures, he desired that the English Church and nation should repudiate their jurisdiction. And yet he did not deny that the English Church had a duty towards Rome, or that Rome had rights which she might justly claim. When the moment for asserting those rights might come, Cranmer's oath bound him not to be wanting. But there were many other claims to be listened to, and to make Rome listen to, first. The King's authority, the imperial freedom of the nation, the prerogatives of the Church of England, needed to be secured; and till this end was accomplished, it was, as Cranmer protested, a matter of form to swear that he would " be faithful and obedient to the blessed Peter, and to the Holy Apostolic Church

of Rome, and to our Lord Clement VII., the Lord Pope, and to his successors canonically coming in," and the rest of it. No oath to uphold " the rights, dignities, privileges, and authority " of the Papacy could in conscience oblige a man to uphold the Papacy in all pretensions that it might choose to make. And at any rate, whatever blame may be thought to attach to Archbishop Cranmer for taking such an oath as only a legal form, attaches also, in a measure, to those prelates who, after hearing his protestations, conferred upon him his sacred order and his pall, and to all who subsequently submitted to him as their metropolitan.

Archbishop Cranmer had only held his crosier for a few days when he proceeded to the business for which he had been chiefly chosen. Consecrated on March 30, he wrote to the King on April 11, petitioning for leave to give a final sentence upon the marriage with Catherine. The letter exists in two forms, both written in the Archbishop's own hand, and both bearing signs of having been sent to the King. Although Convocation had now declared against the validity of the King's marriage, yet, in the country at large, the King's proceedings were regarded with detestation. Cranmer, ready to draw upon himself all the odium, if he could relieve the King of it, wrote as if on his own motion. Doubtless it had been arranged beforehand that he should do so, and it would seem that the letter of request was privately perused by the King or Cromwell, and then rewritten, to ensure that its terms should be perfectly acceptable. After speaking of the way in which the subject was discussed throughout Christendom, and the uncertainty among the ignorant people

of England with regard to the future succession to the throne, Cranmer continues—

" And forasmuch as it hath pleased Almighty God, and your Grace, of your abundant goodness to me showed, to call me, albeit a poor wretch and much unworthy, unto this high and chargeable office of Primate and Archbishop in this your Grace's realm, wherein I beseech Almighty God to grant me His grace so to use and demean myself, as may be standing with His pleasure and the discharge of my conscience, and to the weal of this your Grace's realm: and considering also the obloquy and bruit, which daily doth spring and increase of the clergy of this realm, and specially of the heads and presidents of the same, because they in this behalf do not foresee and provide such convenient remedies as might expel and put out of doubt all such inconveniences, perils, and dangers, as the said rude and ignorant people do speak and talk to be imminent: I, your most humble orator and beadman, am, in consideration of the premises, urgently constrained at the present time most humbly to beseech your most noble Grace, that where the office and duty of the Archbishop of Canterbury, by your and your progenitors' sufferance and grants, is to direct, order, judge, and determine causes spiritual in this your Grace's realm; and because I would be right loth, and also it shall not become me, forasmuch as your Grace is my Prince and Sovereign, to enterprise any part of my office in the said weighty cause touching your Highness, without your Grace's favour and license obtained in that behalf: it may please, therefore, your most excellent Majesty (considerations had to the premises, and to my most bounden duty towards your Highness, your realm, succession,

and posterity, and for the exoneration of my conscience towards Almighty God) to license me, according to mine office and duty, to proceed to the examination, final determination, and judgment in the said great cause touching your Highness." [1]

The Supreme Head, in reply, commended the Archbishop's " good and virtuous intended purpose"; declared that he "recognised no superior in earth, but only God," yet " because ye be, under us, by God's calling and ours, the most spiritual minister of our spiritual jurisdiction within this our realm," would not refuse Cran-mer's " humble request, offer, and towardness," and charged him to proceed with an eye to God and justice only, and not to " any earthly or worldly affection." [2]

The language in which the King spoke of his relation to the primacy was not the language of a Catholic layman ; but even if it galled, which is improbable, it was not openly resented, and Cranmer prepared to act upon it.

"After the Convocation in that behalf," he writes in a letter to a friend abroad, " had determined and agreed according to the former consent of the Universities, it was thought convenient by the King and his learned counsel, that I should repair unto Dunstable, which is within four miles unto Ampthill, where the Lady Catherine keepeth her house, and; there to call her before me to hear the final sentence in the said matter. Notwithstanding," he continues with a somewhat naive surprise, " she would not at all obey thereunto ; for when she was by Dr. Lee cited to appear by a day, she utterly refused the same, saying that inas-

1 Jenkyns i. 22 ; Dixon i. 160.
2 The reply is given in Collier ix. 103.

much as her cause was before the Pope, she would have none other judge, and therefore would not take me for her judge." 1

The Archbishop, notwithstanding, held a court, and, the serving of the summons having been proved, declared the Lady Catherine contumacious. He was informed by the King's counsel (of whom Bishop Gardiner was the chief) that her contumacy precluded her from further monition to appear; and this simplified and accelerated the course of affairs beyond Cranmer's expectation. Henry and Cromwell were urging him on, as if they half distrusted him. " Where I never yet," he wrote back to Cromwell, " went about to injure willingly any man living, I would be loth now to begin with my Prince, and defraud him of his trust in me. And therefore I have used all the expedition that I might conveniently"—that is, with propriety—"use in the King's behalf, and have brought the matter to a final sentence, to be given upon Friday next ensuing. At which time I trust so to endeavour myself further in this behalf as shall become me to do, to the pleasure of Almighty God and the mere truth of the matter." Cranmer excuses himself for not having written before to Cromwell on the subject, and adds—" For divers considerations I do think it right expedient that the matter and the process of the same be kept secret for a time, therefore I pray you to make no relation thereof, as I know well you will not. For if the noble Lady Catherine should by the bruit of this matter in the mouths of the inhabitants of the country, or by her friends or counsel hearing of this bruit, be moved, stirred, counselled, or persuaded, to

1 Jenkyns i. 23.

D

appear before me in the time, or afore the time, of sentence, I should be thereby greatly stayed and let in the process, and the King's grace's counsel here present "—Bishop Gardiner and the rest—" shall be much uncertain what shall be then further done therein. For a great bruit and voice of the people in this behalf might perchance move her to do that thing herein, which peradventure she would not do, if she shall hear little of it." i

This policy of secrecy and haste was not a noble policy; but any just judgment of Cranmer's share in it will be tempered by the recollection that he was at any rate not the author of the policy. It had been pursued throughout by the King's agents, from Wolsey downwards. Cranmer was not even the first to apply it on this particular occasion, but Gardiner and his brother counsel. And as a matter of fact Catherine was not left ignorant of what was being done. She had deliberately chosen not to plead before the Archbishop's court, and must have been well aware what would be the consequences. What Cranmer dreaded was not that Catherine should know; it was that the public should know, and that general indignation should force Catherine to abandon her position, and should induce her after all to acknowledge his tribunal, which would delay matters once more. Cranmer knew well that there were no fresh arguments to be brought forward on Catherine's side, and that all that she could do would be to appeal again from the court of the Metropolitan to that of the Pope—an appeal which the law of England had now by anticipation disallowed. One who is not a friend of Archbishop Cranmer's has the candour to say of his 1 Jenkyns i. 25.

action in this matter, that " no judge, lay or ecclesiastical, at the time, with the exception of More, would have acted otherwise." x Fifteen days were allowed to Catherine in which to repent of her contumacy; but she did not repent. " The morrow after Ascension Day," writes Cranmer, " I gave final sentence therein, how that it was indispensable for the Pope to license any such marriages." 2

That was the light in which Cranmer regarded the matter. He was reviewing an unlawful decision of Pope Julius II., not pronouncing judgment upon an innocent and defenceless woman. The Archbishop was perfectly upright and conscientious in delivering such a sentence ; but it is to be regretted that, in his desire to satisfy the King, and to teach the Papacy a lesson, he should have allowed himself to appear unfeeling towards " the noble Lady Catherine." Those were, indeed, days when men were not disposed to give effusive utterance to their sentiments about one another's political misfortunes; and it is possible to be too hard upon Sir Thomas More's language on the fall of Wolsey, or on the Nun of Kent; or upon Edward VI.'s language on the fall of Somerset, as well as upon that of Cranmer with regard to Catherine. Besides, we possess only scanty fragments of Cranmer's familiar correspondence. But Cranmer could, when he chose, express his sentiments with remarkable freedom, even to Henry VIII. He did so in the case of Ann Boleyn; he did so in the case of Cromwell; it is to be wished that he had done

1 Brewer ii. 189, note. Mr. Brewer is mistaken, however, in what he says. Catherine had already been pronounced contumax, and the fear was lest she should repent of her contumacy.

2 Jenkyns i. 28. It was May 23.

so in the case of that more deserving woman, who had been the victim of the political schemes of Julius, and Ferdinand, and Henry VII., to be afterwards flung away by the so-called husband to whom they had married her.

A really high-minded survey of the situation would have suggested that, although the marriage between Henry and Catherine had been null from the beginning, and could not be made valid by any length of continuance, or by any sanction of ecclesiastical and state authorities, yet the parties to it were bound to each other by honour and affection, and could not rightly consider themselves free to act independently. They were brother and sister, and it was right that they should cease to live as if they were man and wife; but neither of them ought to have thought of entering upon a legitimate marriage without the full consent of the other. Such a view, so far as we know, was not put forward by any of those who voted in Convocation, or Senate-house, or Parliament, for the dissolution of Henry's union with Catherine. If it had been put forward, Henry would certainly never have listened to it; and, indeed, granted the nullity of the first union, no one could have insisted upon prohibiting a second.

Four months at least before Cranmer's sentence was given—perhaps as early as November 14—Henry had been privately married to Ann Boleyn. The marriage had for a while been kept a secret from the Archbishop-Elect. But as soon as he knew of it, he approved it. In his letter from Dunstable to Cromwell, written before his final sentence on the marriage with Catherine had been pronounced, he already speaks of Ann as " the Queen's Grace." 1 A day or two later, 1 Jenkyns i. 26.

he publicly confirmed her marriage; and it only remained, " on the Thursday next before the feast of Pentecost," for him to crown her with extraordinary pomp, " apparelled in a robe of purple velvet, sustained of each side with two bishops, 1 she in her hair," and already " somewhat big with child." 2

It is a wanton insult to the memory of Cranmer to suggest, as Mr. Brewer has done, 3 that he was the author of the monstrous proposition that the Pope should give Henry leave to marry again without pronouncing upon the validity or invalidity of his marriage with Catherine. So low had the moral feeling of Rome fallen, that the Pope listened without abhorrence to the proposal. It is right that this should be borne in mind when men condemn, in unmeasured terms, the conduct of Luther, Melanchthon, and Bucer, who, seven years after Henry's marriage with Ann, gave their sanction to the bigamy of a German prince. The traditions of Rome and the new Gospel light of Germany were alike ready to accommodate themselves to the desires of high-placed sinners. But Cranmer was not infected by any such notions. " You know," he wrote to Osiander, his wife's uncle, after Philip of Hesse had been allowed to enter into that adulterous estate, " how men here always come to ask me to explain what goes on among you ; and there are often things which I can neither deny, nor without a blush confess, and which I cannot think how you can allow. Not to speak of your permitting the sons of great nobles to have concubines, lest old hereditary estates should be broken up through lack of legitimate children, what excuse can you possibly

1 Stokesley and Gardiner. 2 Jenkyns i. 31.

3 Brewer ii. 223.

offer for allowing divorce and remarriage while both the divorced parties are alive, or what is still worse, without any divorce at all, the marriage of a man to more than one wife ? By the teaching of the Apostles, and of Christ Himself, marriage is only of one with one, nor can those who have been thus joined contract new unions except after the death of one or the other partner." He adds, with justice, that it is more like Mahometanism than Christianity to allow such things, and affirms that he would be sorry to have even a slight acquaintance with the professors of the new Gospel, if such are the fruits which it is to produce. 1 It is clear that Cranmer in no way regarded the separation of Henry from Catherine as a divorce, or his marriage with Ann as anything but a first marriage.

News reached England not many weeks after the coronation of Ann, that the Pope was preparing to avenge his slighted authority by such weapons as were possible for him. Henry VIII., on his part, composed, and at length, by the hands of his agent Bonner, delivered to Clement VII., at Marseilles, an appeal from Home to the General Council of Christendom. He advised Cranmer to do the like. It is interesting, in view of the later history of men and things, to read the letter in which Cranmer forwards to the man who was afterwards, by Papal authority, to degrade him, an appeal from the Pope like that which he delivered to Bonner at his degradation. " I stand in dread," wrote the champion of the rights of Canterbury, "lest our holy Father the Pope do intend to make some manner of prejudicial process against me and my Church; and therefore I have provoked from his Holiness to the 1 Jenkyns i. 303.

General Council. Which my provocation, and a pro-curacy under my seal, I do send unto you herewith, desiring you right heartily to have me commended to my Lord of Winchester, 1 and with his advice and counsel to intimate the said provocation after the best manner that his Lordship and you shall think most expedient for me." He adds that even if the King should, percase, forget to write, as he intended, to demand Bonner's services for the Archbishop, Bonner's goodness will make him contented to take this pains at Cranmer's desire alone. 2

The time came when Cranmer had to pay for anything that was unworthy in his conduct with regard to the divorce; and it came long before he suffered at the hands of the injured Catherine's daughter. Three years 'from the time when he crowned Ann as Queen, he received a sudden summons to come up from the country to Lambeth, and not to stir from his house. He found that the Queen had been under trial before the Council, on the most atrocious charges, and had been committed to the Tower. Cranmer was deeply attached to Ann. Forbidden to approach the King in person, he seized his pen and wrote to him one of his simple quivering letters—at once more bold than most men would have dared, and more timid than most men would have cared to write. He wrote, he said, somewhat to "suppress the deep sorrows" of his Grace's heart, and to help him to take them "both patiently and thankfully."

" I am in such perplexity," he said, " that my mind is clean amazed, for I never had better opinion in woman than I had in her, which maketh me think that she 1 Gardiner. 2 Jenkyns i. 71. should not be culpable. And again I think that your Highness would not have gone so far, except she had been surely culpable. Now I think that your Grace best knoweth, that next unto your Grace, I was most bound unto her of all creatures living. Wherefore I most humbly beseech your Grace to suffer me in that which both God's law, nature, and also her kindness bindeth me unto; that is, that I may with your Grace's favour wish and pray for her that she may declare herself inculpable and innocent." He added that if the Queen proved to be guilty, she would deserve hatred in proportion to the scandal which her crimes would bring upon the Gospel which she professed. 1

This letter was written on May 3. Before it was despatched, the Archbishop was summoned to the Star Chamber, and there informed of " such things as" Henry's " pleasure was they should make " him " privy to." The Archbishop did not alter what he had written, but added a postscript, in which he expressed himself as "most bounden" to the King for making such a communication, and " exceedingly sorry that such faults can be proved by 2 the Queen." On May 15 the Queen was found guilty by the peers, and condemned to be burned or beheaded, as the King might choose. With this condemnation Cranmer was not concerned. His part in the tragedy was yet to come. On the day after Ann's trial, he was sent to visit her in the Tower, to receive her confession. The next day, May 17 the King and Queen were cited to appear before him at Lambeth, to answer to certain inquiries for their souls' health. The court sat in the under chapel of the palace. The proceedings occupied but two hours. It 1 Jenkyns i. 163. 2 Against. is asserted in the new Act to regulate the succession l that Ann, probably by her proctor, made damaging admissions before the Archbishop's court; but what those admissions were remained undivulged. On grounds which are to this day unknown, the Archbishop pronounced that the marriage between the King and Ann had never been valid, and that the child born of it, his god-daughter Elizabeth, was illegitimate. Two days later the unhappy Queen was put to death, the Archbishop (if we may trust a Scotch divine who was with him that morning) still believing her to be innocent. 2

Nor was this the last occasion on which Cranmer was required to take part in the miserable business of his master's wives. In four years' time—April, 1540—he set his seal to a document which pronounced yet another of the marriages invalid—that of Anne of Cleves. The grounds in this case are known; and certainly they were shamefully inadequate. The Lady Anne was found to have been precontracted to a prince of the house of Lorraine,—although this was known at the time of the marriage, and had not been considered sufficient to hinder it;—and the King pleaded that he had never inwardly consented to the union, and that he was incapable of fulfilling its conditions,

1 Given in Dixon i. 392.

2 The story is told in Dixon i. 388. Aless affirmed that Cranmer said to him—" She who has been Queen of England on earth will this day become a Queen in heaven." Hook (Life i. 506) thinks that if Cranmer really said this, his conduct was " unspeakably bad." But it was quite possible for him to become convinced that the marriage with Ann was invalid, without being

convinced of the truth of the crimes for which she was beheaded. The two things were entirely separate. Aless's narrative, however, is evidently inaccurate in some particulars, and seems very improbable altogether,

and had never attempted to fulfil them—though for six months their life together had, in the world's eye, been that of married people. It is too probable that (as Burnet says) l Archbishop Cranmer had not now "courage enough to swim against the stream," which was fast sweeping Cromwell to execution ; but it must be remembered, in mitigation of judgment upon him, that he would have stood absolutely alone, if he had refused to act as he did. Not only had the Convocation of both provinces reported to Parliament that the marriage was void, and Parliament had ratified the decision—Bishop Gardiner taking a leading part in this case as in the case of Catherine—but the Lady Anne herself perfectly acquiesced in the truth of the allegations made, and was quite content to abide by the decision. When afterwards the Duke of Cleves was anxious to effect " a reconciliation " of the matrimony, and to obtain the Archbishop's support, Cranmer utterly refused to give him any encouragement, and instantly reported the occurrence direct to the King. 2

It was only some year and a half after Henry's marriage with Anne of Cleves, that it became Cranmer's duty to inform the King, who had lately given solemn thanks for the happiness of his marriage with Catherine Howard, that he had received intelligence of the gravest kind regarding the Queen's moral conduct before her marriage. His compassionate heart was torn when the task was assigned to him of extracting from the young Queen an account of what had passed in those days between her and Dereham. It seems from his language to Henry VIII., that he visited her

1 Hist. Eef. iii. Appendix 9.

2 Jenkyns i. 312.

time after time, 1 and was kept whole days at the distressing work. " At my repair unto the Queen's Grace, I found her in such lamentation and heaviness, as I never saw no creature ; so that it would have pitied any man's heart in the world to have looked upon her; and in that vehement rage she continued, as they informed me which be about her, from my departure from her to my return again; and then I found her, as I do suppose, far entered toward a frenzy." 2 At length she was partially calmed by a message which he was commissioned to bring her from the King, promising her mercy if she would make a full confession. The promise, however, was delusive; and the fifth wife, like the second, perished by the axe on Tower Green.

1 "Now I do use her thus ; when I do see her in any such extreme brayds, I do travail with her to know the cause ; . . .. and so I did at that time."

2 Jenkyns i. 308.

CHAPTER II

CRANMER AND PUBLIC AFFAIRS UNDER HENRY

THE divorce of Catherine of Aragon was extremely unpopular in the country. Not only were men's generous impulses on the side of the oppressed Queen, but all that was most conservative in religion espoused her cause, which was practically that of the Pope. While the matter was still under discussion, sermons against the divorce were constantly preached in the churches. One of the first acts of the new Primate was to inhibit all manner of preaching in his own diocese, and to require his suffragans to do much the same. It is said that Cranmer became so much detested for his action in the matter of the divorce as to require special protection when, in 1533, he began to visit the city and diocese of Canterbury. 1

The hostile feeling against the King's proceedings had found a centre in the metropolitical city, round the person of a nun of St. Sepulchre's, Elizabeth Barton, the " Holy Maid of Kent." This woman, belonging to that well-known class of religionists, of whom it is difficult to say how far they really believe in their own inspiration, had acquired a strange influence as the

1 Hook i. 479. Hook has, however, made too much of the Injunction to which he refers, which seems to be quite general in character.

utterer of prophecies. In some of these she had denounced judgment upon the King, who was, according to her, barely to survive if he should put away Catherine and marry another, and from that moment forth would have no claim to his subjects' allegiance. Henry's was not a reign in which such speeches were left to refute themselves; and real danger might be thought to connect itself with the Nun of Kent, because of the high character and position of many of those who were brought in contact with her. She had been received by Wolsey and by Warham, and by the King himself. Fisher and More had both conversed with her. The powerful convent of Canterbury Cathedral supplied her with confessors and directors from amongst its principal and most learned members. She was in active correspondence with the Charterhouses of London and Sheen, with the Brigittines of Sion and the Observants of Greenwich and Canterbury, in short, with all that was most respected in the monastic religion of the day. Her influence was real, and widely felt. " I think," wrote the Archbishop to a friend, "that she did marvellously stop the going forward of the King's marriage, insomuch that she wrote letters to the Pope calling upon him in God's behalf to stop it. She had also communication with my Lord Cardinal and with my Lord of Canterbury, my predecessor, in the matter, and in mine opinion with her feigned visions and godly threatenings stayed them very much." 1

It was clear that Elizabeth Barton could not be allowed to continue thus. About midsummer, 1533, Cranmer wrote to the Prioress of St. Sepulchre's—

" Sister Prioress, in my hearty wise I commend me 1 Jenkyns i. 81.

unto you. And so likewise will that you do repair unto me to my manor of Otteforde, and bring with you your nun which was some time at Courtupstrete, against Wednesday next coming: and that ye fail not herein in any wise." 1

A letter from the Dean of the Arches tells Cromwell how the Archbishop at this interview humoured the nun, by granting her leave to go for a week to Court-upstreet in order that a new trance might throw light upon matters which the last had left uncertain. " My Lord doth yet but dally with her, as [if] he did believe her every word." 2 Whether to Cranmer himself, or shortly after at the more terrible tribunal of Cromwell, the unhappy woman confessed, or was thought to have confessed, that her visions were a tissue of impostures; "that she never had vision in all her life, but all that ever she said was feigned of her own imagination, only to satisfy the minds of them the which resorted unto her, and to obtain worldly praise." 3 She and her accomplices were made to do public penance at St. Paul's Cross and at Canterbury Cathedral; 4 but the ecclesiastical penalty was not deemed sufficient. A bill of attainder was brought in against them early in the following year; and on April 20, Elizabeth Barton and her principal associates were hanged and beheaded at Tyburn.

The dismay was great at Canterbury; and Cranmer, at the request of the Prior and Convent of Christ Church, wrote to the King on their behalf. He found

1 Jenkyns i. 43.
2 Calendar of State Papers vi. 967.
3 Cranmer to Hawkyns, Jenkyns i. 82.
4 Chronicle of St. Augustine's, Canterbury, in Narratives of the Reformation p. 280.

them, he said, "as conformable and reformable as any number" with whom he had ever communed. They lamented that any of their congregation should so have ordered himself. Only few had been at all concerned with the nun, " and they, with the exception of Dr. Bocking, who misled them, men of young years and of less knowledge and experience." The Prior and " his brethren, the saddest and seniors of the house, with all the other young sort," regarded the King's pleasure as greatly as anything else in the world. They offered the King a present of two or three hundred pounds—worth at least ten times as much now—in hopes that he would be gracious to them, and not visit the fault of a few upon the whole company. Cranmer most humbly besought his Highness to be gracious and merciful unto them, " the rather for my poor intercession;" 1 and his request was granted, at least for the moment.

Two of the noblest names in English history had been inserted in the bill against the Nun of Kent— the names of Bishop Fisher and Sir Thomas More. More had little difficulty in clearing himself of any complicity with " the lewd nun," " that housewife," " a false deceiving hypocrite," as with somewhat unnecessary severity he terms her. 2 Fisher was found guilty of "misprision of treason," for not having revealed the nun's disloyal utterances, and was condemned to pay a fine. It was the first serious attempt on the part of Cromwell and the King to be rid of the two chief opponents of their proceedings : if Archbishop Cranmer's advice had been taken, it would have been the last.

1 Jenkyns i. 76.
2 Bridgett's More p. 323 (2nd ed.) ; Gasquet's English Monasteries i. 143.

The Act of Succession, passed at the end of March 1534, entailed the Crown upon the children of Ann Boleyn, declaring the King's former marriage to have been contrary to the laws of God, and therefore not to be made good by any dispensation. " God give grace," said More to his son-in-law, when first the marriage with Ann was made public, "that these matters within a while be not confirmed with oaths." This was precisely what the Act of Succession required. It did not contain any form of oath; but a form was soon provided by letters patent, which not only asserted what was asserted in the Act of Parliament and its preamble, but also renounced "any other (besides the King's Majesty) within this realm, or foreign authority, prince, or potentate," and repudiated any oath which might have been previously taken to any other person or persons. 1 Commissioners were appointed to administer the oath; and chief among them was the Archbishop of Canterbury.

Sir Thomas More has left us, in a letter to his daughter, a vivid description of the scene at Lambeth, when he appeared there to be sworn, before the Archbishop, the Lord Chancellor, the Secretary Cromwell, and the Abbot of Westminster. When he told the commissioners that he " would not deny to swear to the succession," but that he could not take the oath as it stood, U I was commanded," he says, "to go down into the garden, and thereupon I tarried in the old burned chamber that looketh into the garden, and would not go down because of the heat. In that time I saw Mr. Dr. Latimer come into the garden, and there walked he with divers other doctors and chaplains 1 Dixon i. 205.

of my Lord of Canterbury. And very merry I saw him, for he laughed, and took one or twain about the neck so handsomely, that if they had been women, I would have weened he had been waxen wanton." He saw one clergyman, for refusing the oath, " gentlemanly sent straight unto the Tower " ; the rest, who swore, including almost all the clergy of London, "sped apace to their great comfort; so far forth that Master Vicar of Croydon, either for gladness, or for dry ness, or else that it might be seen quod ille notios erat pontifici, went to my Lord's buttery bar and called for drink valde familiariter" When More was called up again, a notable conversation took place between him and the Archbishop. "My Lord of Canterbury, taking hold upon that that I said, that I condemned not the consciences of them that swear, said unto me that it appeared well, that I did not take it for a very sure thing and a certain that I might not lawfully swear it, but rather as a thing uncertain and doubtful. ' But then said my Lord, you know for a certainty that you be bound to obey your Sovereign Lord, your King. And therefore are you bound to leave off the doubt of your unsure conscience in refusing the oath, and take the sure way in obeying of your Prince, and swear it ... This argument seemed me suddenly so subtle, and namely with such authority coming out of so noble a prelate's mouth, that I could again answer nothing thereto, but only that I thought myself I might not well do so." 1

When Bishop Fisher came before the commissioners, he asked leave to read and study the oath before giving his reply. They allowed him a few days for 1 Bridgett's More p. 354.

consideration; and then he told them that he was ready to swear to a part of it, but not to all. They "answered that the King would by no means like of any kind of exceptions or conditions ; ' And therefore/ said my Lord of Canterbury, 'you must answer directly to our question, whether you will swear the oath or no.' 1 Then said my Lord of Rochester, ' I do absolutely refuse the oath.' "

Archbishop Cranmer, however, was too desirous for the safety of the illustrious malcontents to allow these answers of theirs to be final. He wrote to Cromwell earnestly begging that they should be allowed to swear after their own fashion. " I doubt not but you do right well remember that my Lord of Rochester and Master More were contented to be sworn to the Act of the King's succession, but not to the preamble of the same. What was the cause of their refusal thereof I am uncertain, and they would by no means express the same. 2 Nevertheless, it must needs be, either the diminution of the authority of the Bishop of Rome, or else the reprobation of the King's first pretensed matrimony. But if they do obstinately persist in their opinions of the preamble, yet meseemeth it should not be refused, if they will be sworn to the very Act of Succession; so that they will be sworn to maintain the same against all powers and potentates." He urged the good effect which their swearing would produce upon the "Princess Dowager and the Lady Mary," upon the Emperor and other friends. He pleaded that if such men should say that the new succession was

1 Van Ortroy p. 285.

2 They had not given their reasons, lest the statement of them should be treated as an act of high treason.

good and according to God's laws, no one within the realm would once reclaim against it. Some persons, he said, could not alter from their opinions of the pretensed marriage, or of the Bishop of Rome's authority; their consciences were indurate and invert-iblc; they had once said their minds, and felt that if they now varied therefrom, their fame and estimation would be distained for ever; but if they could but be brought to acknowledge the succession itself, it should be amplected and embraced, and that this end would be greatly furthered by the consent of the Bishop and More. He added that if the King pleased, " their said oaths might be suppressed," except when and where the publishing of the same might be serviceable. 1

Cranmer's prudent letter was laid before the King; but the King " in no wise willed but that they should be sworn as well to the preamble as to the Act. Wherefore Cromwell said, "his Grace specially trusteth that ye will in no wise attempt or move him to the contrary." 2 The effort was unavailing; but it is satisfactory to know that the blood of the two most famous martyrs of the reign was in no way to be laid to the charge of the Archbishop.

Nor did he fail to strive likewise to save the scarcely less noble, if not so celebrated martyrs, the sight of whom, as they went out to execution, moved Sir

1 It is questionable what Cranmer meant by the last sentence. People generally suppose that he meant that it might be given out that they had taken the oath, without letting it be known that the oath in their case was taken with a diti'erence. Certainly such advice would not be to Cranmer's honour. But it is at least possible that Cranmer meant that it need not everywhere be blazed abroad that they had taken the oath at all : the great thing was to get them quietly through.

2 Bridgett's Fisher p. 279.

Thomas More to such envious self-contempt. 1 Cranmer had at an earlier time been on good terms with Austin Webster, Prior of the Charterhouse of Axholme; 2 and when Webster, with Reynold of Sion and others, had been attainted of high treason for clinging to "the usurped power of the Bishop of Rome," Cranmer was surprised. Webster had promised him never to "meddle for the defence of that opinion." It moved the Archbishop's pity that men so learned in Scriptures and Doctors should suffer by their ignorance on this point. "If there be none other offence laid against them than this one," he wrote to Cromwell, " it will be much more for the conversion of all the fautors thereof, after mine opinion, that their consciences may be clearly averted from the same by communication of sincere doctrine, and so they to publish it likewise to the world, than by the justice of the law to suffer in such ignorance. And if it would please the King's Highness to send them unto me, I suppose I could do veiy much with them in this behalf." 3 It does not appear that the sanguine Archbishop was permitted to make his experiment; it is certain that the two men for whom he pleaded so earnestly were horribly put to death.

Not loKg before the slaughter of the Carthusians and their associates, a step had been taken which was full of terrible cpnsequence for the Church of England. It was the practical delegation of the King's newly declared headship to a vicar-general, in the person of Thomas Cromwell,

It migho have been thought that the declaration of

1 Bridge tt's More p. 404. 2 See Jenkyns i. 127.

3 Ibid, i; 134.

the independence of the national Church as against Rome would have added dignity to the See of Canterbury ; and perhaps at first it was the intention of the King that this should be the case. Early in 1534 there was a kind of partition between the Archbishop and the King of the prerogatives which had been acquired in the course of ages by the Pope; and the power of granting licenses and dispensations, such as had before been only obtainable from Rome, fell to the Archbishop. He even conferred the pall upon the successor of Lee in the northern primacy with an impressive ceremonial in his chapel at Lambeth. 1 He had at all times possessed the rights inherent in a primatial and metropolitical see; and in that capacity Cranmer proceeded to make a visitation of his province. At the time that his monition on the subject was issued to the premier diocese of London, the old official style had not been altered. Cranmer was designated in the instrument as Legate of the Apostolic See. Visitations were always unpopular, and in those days were costly to the visited. Bishop Stokesley resisted the visitation. He and his Chapter protested—the penalties of a Praemunire might be hanging over them—that they could not recognise the Archbishop as Legate, and they appealed to the King. But the King upheld the Archbishop, and the visitation went forward. Cranmer turned to the great diocese of Winchester. Bishop Gardiner withstood him likewise. He urged with some reason that Warham had visited him only five years before : and besides—Cranmer having meanwhile

1 Strype's Cranmer ch. xxix. See the paper by [Bi.-hop] Stubbs in the Gentleman's Magazine for November 1860, p. 522 ; cp. also p. 648.

discarded the legatine title—that it was contrary to the royal supremacy for any subject to style himself Primate of all England.

The objection called forth one of Cranmer's most characteristic letters. Already whatever love may once have existed between the old Cambridge acquaintances was fast vanishing. Cranmer wrote to Cromwell, then still secretary, that Gardiner was endeavouring to advance his own cause under pretence of the King's. " Ye know," he said, " the man lacketh neither learning in the law, neither witty invention, no craft to set forth his matters to the best." The Bishop of Rome, he urged—with some logical force, if his premiss were allowed to be exact—had formerly been taken for Supreme Head, and yet had a great number of primates under him, without derogation to his authority; why should it not be so with the King? All the bishops in England would gladly have conspired with the Pope to take away the primatial title, so that they might have been all equal together, if the Pope had wished to abolish it in the interest of his supreme authority.

" All this notwithstanding," he pursued, " if the Bishops of this realm pass no more of [1] their names, styles, and titles, than I do of mine, the King's Highness shall soon order the matter between us all. ... I pray God never be merciful unto me at the general judgment, if I perceive in my heart that I set more by any title, name, or style that I write than I do by the paring of an apple, farther than it shall be to the setting forth of God's word and will. Yet will I not utterly excuse me herein; for God must be my judge, who knoweth the bottom of my heart, and so do not I [1] Care no more for.

myself; but I speak for so much as I do feel in my heart; for many evil affections lie lurking there, and will not lightly be espied. But yet I would not gladly leave any just thing at the pleasure and suit of the Bishop of Winchester, he being none otherwise affectionate unto me than he is. Even at the beginning first of Christ's profession, Diotrephes desired gerere primatum in ecclesia : and since, he hath had more successors than all the Apostles had, of whom have come all these glorious titles, styles, and pomps into the Church. But I would that I, and all my brethren the Bishops, would leave all our styles, and write the style of our offices, calling ourselves Apostolos Jesu Christi; so that we took not upon us the name vainly, but were so even in deed ; so that we might order our diocese in such sort that neither paper, parchment, lead, nor wax, but the very Christian conversation of the people, might be the letters and seals of our offices, as the Corinthians were unto Paul, to whom he said, Litterae nostrae et signa Apostolatus nostri vos estis" [1]

The extent of Cranmer's deference to royal authority was soon put to the test by Cromwell's new appointment. He became Vicar-General of the King in 1535. The instrument which appointed him was in truth a terrible document. It laid the entire system of the Church of England at the mercy of the Vicegerent. He was empowered not only to visit, in person or by deputy, all ecclesiastical bodies and persons, but also, amongst other things, to suspend or deprive, to summon synods, to legislate, to direct the elections of prelates, and to annul them if he thought proper. An attempt was indeed made to distinguish between the prerogatives [1] Jenkyns i. 136.

which were bestowed upon the bishops by Divine commission in the Scriptures, and those which they exercised by grace of the King, and in his stead; but never was the English Church submitted to such an usurpation as at Cromwell's appointment. And to add insult to injury, the preface to the fulsome document stated (in language which was perhaps aimed chiefly at the Pope, but at any rate seemed to strike the higher clergy of the realm), that the appointment of a Vicar-General of the King was made necessary by the self-seeking, the indolence, the licentious bad example of those who claimed to govern the Church, by which the Bride of Christ had been so disfigured that her Spouse could barely recognise her. 1

In June of the year following that which saw the appointment made, Convocation was summoned. At its first session for purposes of deliberation, Dr. William Petre appeared in the Upper House, and claimed to preside over it as the representative of the Vicegerent. Many, at the time, no doubt, must have felt surprise and indignation, as historians of a later date have felt it; but there is no record of any protest having been made. The Popes had accustomed men to seeing lawful authorities overridden; and if Cranmer's theory of the transference of the Supreme Headship from the Pope to the King was true, it was as innocent for the King's deputy to take precedence of Cranmer in the Convocation of Canterbury as it had been for Wolsey to take precedence of Warham. Stokesley and Gardiner were as much committed to the principle involved as Cranmer himself was. In the extreme form, however, the insult was not repeated. Cromwell presided in 1 The document is given in Collier ix. p. 119.

person at the next session. This was bad enough ; but it was not quite so offensive as to send his proctor to preside in the venerable assembly.

But the main purpose of Cromwell's appointment was not to take down the pride of prelates and convocations. It was to bring money into the King's exchequer. His first act was to inhibit, through Cranmer, all archbishops and bishops from visiting their dioceses and provinces, and in fact to suspend all ordinary jurisdictions whatever, until a visitation by the Supreme Head should have been carried through. Most of the monasteries had always been exempted from episcopal jurisdiction, and when the Papal authority was swept away and divided between the Crown and the Primate, it had been expressly enacted that neither the Archbishop of Canterbury nor any one else should have power to visit them. The purpose of this enactment was clear. A royal visitation of the monasteries was the prelude to their suppression; and the King and Cromwell did not wish any ecclesiastic to be able to interpose a shield between the monasteries and the spoiler.

A Life of Cranmer is not required to narrate the shameful and wasteful process by which the religious houses of England were broken up and their property squandered. It was not Craomer's doing, and he had no power to check it. Sympathy with the monastic system he probably had none. On occasion he spoke of monks and friars with all the scorn which was common among seculars. He thought that many of the Observants were " wolves in sheep's skins." l He trusted that their " irreligious religion " might be " extinguished " 1 Jenkyns i. 181.

at Canterbury as well as elsewhere. 1 Bat he approved of the original intention of such foundations. 2 Quite a number of his earlier letters are addressed to " Brother Abbots" and " Sister Prioresses," and show him to be on pleasant terms with them. In the house of the Black Friars at Cambridge he knows " men of good study, living, learning, and judgment; and pity it were," he thinks, " but that they should have such a head and ruler as is of like qualities." 3 He recommends two Benedictines as candidates for the vacant Priory of Worcester, and says, " I know no religious men in England of that habit that be of better learning, judgment, conversation, and all qualities meet for an head and master of an house." 4 Cranmer would probably never have stirred for a dissolution of the monasteries. When others did so, he made no personal gain by it. Though he occasionally begs Cromwell for small grants of monastic property for friends and dependents, he asks nothing for himself. The few pieces of monastic property which he acquired were by way of exchange, and at ruinous cost. 5 However pleased he may have been for some reasons to see the dissolution, the way in which the plunder was employed was a deep disappointment to him, as it was also to Latimer. " I was ever hitherto cold," he writes to the Vicegerent, " but now I am in a heat with the cause of religion"—that is, of monasticism— " which goeth all contrary to mine expect-

1 Jenkyns i. 174.

2 " The beginning of prebendaries was no less purposed for the maintenance of good learning and good conversation of living, than religious men were." To Cromwell: Jenkyns i. 292.

3 Jenkyns i. 120. 4 Ibid. i. 144.

6 See Dixon i. 333, 396 ; ii. 151. But compare Narratives of Eeformation p. 263.

ation, if it be as the fame goeth; wherein I would wonder fain break my mind unto you, and, if you please, I will come to such place as you shall appoint for the purpose." 1 But Cromwell had no desire for his counsel, and the Archbishop was probably obliged to keep it to himself. There was one monastery with which it is especially interesting to trace Cranmer's relations. Though a secular and a married man, he was himself, by virtue of his archbishopric, the head of the great convent of Christ Church at Canterbury. It and its Prior were to him " the Prior and Convent of my Church." 2 Its monks were to him, in a peculiar sense " my brethren." He writes to the Prior about " your brothern and mine." When he first came to the see the convent bore the expense of his enthronement banquet. 3 He was in great difficulties about money at the time; and he "showed his necessity" to the convent, "thinking of good congruence he might be more bolder of them, and they likewise of him, than to attempt or prove any foreign friends." He promised that he would so recompense them as they should be well contented and pleased withal. 4 How warmly, in fulfilment of this promise, he espoused their cause at the time of their troubles over the Nun, has already been told. It was then their turn to plead poverty. They could not offer the King as much as they would have wished. " Besides the ornaments of the Church, and some plate that the Prior and certain officeis hath, this monastery is not aforehand," he tells the King, " but in debt divers ways." He prays his Highness to send them " some comfortable word or letter for their comfortation in this their great

1 Jeiikyns i. 162. 2 Ibid. i. 76.

3 Hook i. p. 460. 4 Jeiikyns i. 57.

pensiveness and dolour." 1 When the visitation of the monasteries began, a great show was made of restoring the strict discipline of former days. Amongst other things, the monks were forbidden, on any pretext whatever, to go beyond the precincts. Hereupon the Archbishop wrote to Cromwell to intercede for a relaxation of the rules on behalf of one of the great officers of the House, the Cellarer, whose health would suffer by the confinement. The Archbishop was anxious for the consequences not only for the Cellarer himself, but for the House. " The said monastery should lack many commodities, which daily do grow and increase by his policy and wisdom by his provision abroad; for he is the only jewel and housewife of that house." 2 Cranmer was appealed to for an explanation of the new regulations that had been laid down for the dismissal of the younger monks, but prudently referred the questions to headquarters. 3

In spite of his solicitude for the welfare of the House, it is not likely that the Archbishop was looked upon with favour by more than a small section of the brethren. They may perhaps have been English-minded enough to bear it with equanimity, when Cranmer, thinking Canterbury to be more backward than any other place in his diocese, preached in his cathedral two sermons (which he confesses to have been " long " ones) to prove that the Pope's authority was but an usurpation, and that the King was, by God's law, the Supreme Head of the Church of England. We hear of no refusals to swear to the Supreme Headship at Canterbury. But there was a cause of disagreement

1 Jenkyns i. 77. 2 Ibid. i. 148.

3 Ibid. i. 155.

which touched nearer home. The glory of the great convent was all bound up with the shrine of St. Thomas. It must have struck horror into the heart of every monk of Christ Church when he heard that St. Thomas' successor and namesake had written to the Vicegerent on August 18, 1538, to say that he greatly suspected the martyr's blood in the cathedral to be " but a feigned thing, made of some red ochre or of such like matter," and had begged that his chaplains might be commissioned " to try and examine that and all other like things there." 1 Already, in the year before, Cranmer had done a deed which awoke consternation even in the rival convent of St. Austin's, where the name of St. Thomas was less cherished. Convocation, acting in obedience to royal stimulus, had abrogated all but certain specified festivals during harvest time and term time. Cranmer, who found the people of his diocese obstinately observing these abrogated days, and who expostulated with Cromwell for allowing them to be still observed at Court, 2 was minded himself to set a striking example of compliance. Among the festivals which had not been retained was that of the Translation of St. Thomas, on July 7th. The day before had long been observed, like the eves of other great holidays, as a solemn fast. But in that "same year," writes the astonished chronicler of St. Augustine's, " the Archbishop of Canterbury did not fast on St. Thomas' Even, but did eat flesh, and did sup in his parlour with his family, which was never seen before in all the country." 3 After this it was to little purpose that Cranmer devoted half the following Lent to " reading the Epistle of St.

1 Jenkyns i. 262. 2 Ibid. i. 201.
3 Narratives of the Reformation p. 285.

Paul to the Hebrews in the Chapter House " of the cathedral monastery. 1 He must have been heard by an unwilling and offended audience.

The Prior of the convent throughout all those anxious days was Thomas Goldwell. 2 He was, at the beginning of Cranmer's reign, "a man of great simplicity, and void of malice," as far as the Archbishop could judge. 3 But in course of time a mutual suspicion arose between the two men. Cranmer complained that the Prior, contrary to promise, had behaved badly to his physician; 4 that he did not regard the King's injunctions, professing to have dispensation to display the relics, on St. Blaise's day, after the King had forbidden such exhibitions; 5 that he had readmitted to the convent a monk who had run away in suspicious circumstances, and who was supposed to have spent his time at Rome. 6 A short while before the dissolution Cranmer heard a rumour that Cromwell intended to depose Goldwell and put another Prior in his place. It caused him little regret. He begged that, if the report were true, Goldwell's office might be conferred on Dr. Richard Thornden, the Warden of the Manors of the house. He described him as " a man of right honest

1 Narratives of the Reformation p. 286.
2 Hook (Cranmer ii. 10) is in error when he identifies Cranmer's Prior with the great builder of Christ Church gate and of the central Tower, the conductor of Colet and Erasmus. This was his predecessor, Thomas Goldstone. Thomas Goldwell, however, was in his way a builder too. He built a pier at Dover " to his great charge and cost." Narratives of the Reformation p. 283.
3 Jenkyns ii. 77. 4 Ibid. i. 223. 6 Ibid. i. 182.
6 Ibid. i. 254. Mr. Dixon i. 330 asserts that the Prior of the Black Friars who preached against Cranmer at Canterbury did so at Prior Goldwell's instigation, and in the cathedral pulpit. I cannot find any authority for these two statements. Certainly Cranmer himself does not suggest it (Jenkyns i. 170).

behaviour, clean living, good learning, good judgment, without superstition, very tractable, and as ready to set forward his Prince's causes, as no man more of his coat." His commendation of Thornden ends with what appears to be an innuendo against the aged Gold well—" I am moved to write to your Lordship in this behalf, inasmuch as I consider what a great commodity I shall have, if such one be promoted to the said office that is a right honest man and of his qualities; and I insure your Lordship the said room requireth such one; as krioweth God." 1 It was not the first time that Cranmer had written in support of Thornden; 2 and Prior Goldwell had some reason to be jealous of the Warden's influence. When the time came for the conversion of the Prior and Convent into Dean and Chapter, the old man piteously entreated Cromwell to make him Dean. He heard that the commissioners who were to effect the change were about to visit the cathedral," of the which commission my Lord of Canterbury, as I hear, shall be the chief, who is not so good lord unto me as I would he were. Wherefore, without your especial lordship, I suppose my Lord of Canterbury will put me to as much hindrance as he can; and also I have heard of late that my brother, the Warden of the Manors, Dr. Thornden, is called in my Lord of Canterbury's house, ' Dean of Christ Church in Canterbury.' This office of Dean by the favour of your good Lordship I trusted to have had, and as yet trust to have. I have been Prior of the said church above 22 years, wherefore it would be much displeasure to me in my age to be put from my chamber and lodging." 3 The Prior did not obtain his desire.

1 Jenkyns i. 239. 2 Ibid. i. 148.
3 Gasquet English Monasteries ii. 474.

He was offered one of the prebends of the new foundation, which he refused, and retired upon a pension of £80 a year—equivalent to nearly £1000 now. But he succeeded in putting a spoke in Thornden's wheel. Thornden became a prebendary, and, after a while, Bishop Suffragan of Dover; but the deanery was given to another, and Cranmer had reason to think very differently afterwards of the man whose advancement he had pressed. 1

The Archbishop was not entirely satisfied with what Goldwell calls the " change of religion" which took place in his cathedral. There was a magnificence about the new scheme which might well make the royal founder feel satisfied with himself. He thought that the perusal of it would convince the King of Scotland of the godliness of his proceedings. 2 A hundred and sixty-eight persons constituted the new body, headed by a Provost, twelve prebendaries, and six preachers. When the scheme was sent to Cranmer for his opinion, he evinced no great admiration for the scale of payments . on which the new establishment was framed. " Surely, my Lord," he wrote to Cromwell, " I think that it will be a very substantial and godly foundation. Nevertheless, in my opinion, the Prebendaries, which be allowed £40 a piece yearly, might be altered to a more expedient use. Having experience both in times past, and also in our days, how the said sect of prebendaries have not only spent their time in much idleness, and their substance in superfluous belly cheer, I think it not

1 Gasquet is wrong in saying that Thornden became Dean. Nicholas Wotton was the first Dean of Canterbury under Henry VIII. Dr. Crome, however, not Dr. Thornden, was Cranmer's final candidate (Jenkyns i. 294).
2 Jenkyns i. 291.

to be a convenient state or degree to be maintained and established." A prebendary, he said, was commonly "neither a learner, nor teacher, but a good viander." They were always intriguing to get their own way in the college. When learned men were admitted to such rooms, they were apt to desist from their good and godly studies, and all other Christian exercise of preaching and teaching. Wherefore he wished that not only the name of a prebendary were exiled the King's foundations, but also the superfluous conditions of such persons. " To say the truth," he continued, in a style which soon after became very cheap, " it is an estate which St. Paul, reckoning up the degrees and estates allowed in his time, could not find in the Church of Christ." He thought, instead of the twelve wealth\'7d' prebendaries, it would be better to have "twenty divines at £10 a piece, like as it is appointed to be at Oxford and Cambridge; and forty students in the tongues and sciences and French, to have ten marks apiece." In this way the readers, or professors, contemplated in the scheme, would have better audiences ; for assuredly the twelve prebendaries would be too busy " making of good cheer" to attend their lectures.

A prebendary of Canterbury, who reveres at a distance of three centuries and a half the name of Archbishop Cranmer, may regret that he had so bad an opinion of his " sect," and may hope that it would have been altered if he could have foreseen the subsequent history of the cathedral body. But it is a pleasure to observe that Cranmer's design was to increase, and not diminish, the number of priests attached to his cathedral; and that if the scheme, with his alterations, had taken effect, Canterbury would have

become a very great educational centre, if not a very rich one.

Another part of the educational scheme in connexion with the cathedral drew out the zeal of Archbishop Cranmer in a manner which no generous heart can fail to admire. The story is told by his secretary Morice, who was evidently present at the scene which he describes. When the commissioners were engaged in electing the sixty scholars of the new King's School, " more than one or two" would have " none admitted but younger brethren and gentlemen's sons: as for other, husbandmen's children, they were more meet, they said, for the plough and to be artificers than to occupy the place of the learned sort."

It was indeed the characteristic of the age of Henry to plunder the patrimony of the poor for the sake of enriching the rich. But Cranrner did not share the fashionable views of his day. "Poor men's children," he said, " are many times endued with more singular gifts of nature, which are also the gifts of God—as with eloquence, memory, apt pronuntiation, sobriety, with such like—and also commonly more given to apply their study, than is the gentleman's son, delicately educated." To the plea that ploughmen were as much needed in the commonwealth as any other set of men, and that therefore it was best to keep the ploughman's son to the plough, the Archbishop replied "that utterly to exclude the poor man's sons from the benefit of learning, as though they were unworthy to have the gifts of the Holy Ghost bestowed upon them as well as upon others," was " as much as to say that Almighty God should not be at liberty to bestow His great gifts of grace but as we shall appoint them, to be employed according to our

fancy." God, he said, "giveth His gifts, both of learning and other perfections in all sciences, unto all kind and states of people indifferently: even so doth He many times withdraw from them and their posterity again those beneficial gifts, if they be not thankful." He said that it was as vain as the Babel-builders' work to attempt "to shut up into a straight corner the bountiful grace of the Holy Ghost." God would provide that the offspring of the best born children should become " most unapt to learn, and very dolts " ; he himself had seen no small number of them " very dull and without all manner of capacity. I take it," he pursued, " that none of us all here, being gentlemen born (as I think), but had our beginning that way from a low and base parentage—and through the benefit of learning and other civil knowledge all gentle[folk] ascend to their estate." Feats of arms, they replied, and martial acts, had been the chief means of such advancement: to which the Archbishop retorted—" As though the noble captain was always unfurnished of good learning and knowledge to persuade and dissuade his army ! To conclude, if the gentleman's son be apt to learning, let him be admitted; if not apt, let the poor man's child apt enter his room." 1

To have been put into a secondary place in the Church of England by a lay Vicegerent, woke no resentment in the placid and unselfasserting mind of Cranmer. A curious friendship sprang up between him and Thomas Cromwell—a friendship which may be compared to the friendship between Matthew Parker and Burleigh, or, more distantly, to that between Laud and Stafford. It was the friendship of two men 1 Narratives of the Reformation p. 273,

thrown together by common official work, and, in the main, animated in the performance of it by the same ideas. It is a pity that we have not, as in the case of the two later Primates, both sides of the correspondence preserved. While Cromwell kept every trifling note which he received from the Archbishop, Cranmer either did not keep the letters of Cromwell, or they are lost. Enough remains, however, to show the contrast between the characters of the two men—the layman reserved, yet passionate, seldom asking or accepting advice, self-reliant; the priest sanguine, open-hearted and communicative, afraid of giving offence or pain, always assuming that his correspondent's sympathies are on his side, and apparently without a will of his own, except where principle is concerned. Where principle is concerned Cranmer speaks out. There is a fine note of firmness in his first letter of any importance to Cromwell, written a few weeks after his consecration. Cromwell had asked him to promise to appoint a nominee of his to a priory.

" Master Cromwell," he answers, " I am entirely resolved to prefer to the same office, and all such other when the same shall be void, some such one person as was professed in the same house, et sic de eodem gremio, if any such shall be found apt and meet. If there be none so apt and meet in the said house, then I will be glad to provide the most meetest that can be found in any other place, of the same rule, habit, and religion. Of whose sufficiency and ability I ought, if I do my office and duty, to have good experience and knowledge myself, afore that I will admit or prefer him: and for as much as I do not know the person whom ye would prefer to this office, I pray you that I may be ascertained

of his name, and of the place where he doth demore. That done, I will hereafter make you such further answer as I trust ye shall be pleased withal." The fact that Cromwell's letter was brought by his candidate in person made Cranmer wish " to take longer respite in this behalf. Ye do know," he continues, " what ambition and desire of promotion is in men of the Church, and what indirect means they do use to obtain their purpose; and I remit to your wisdom and judgment what an unreasonable thing it is for a man to labour for his own promotion spiritual." 1

Cromwell sues to him for a dispensation on behalf of a man who wishes to marry the niece of his deceased wife—a degree which was not prohibited by the latest statute on the subject.

" Surely, my Lord," is the reply, " I would gladly accomplish your request herein, if the word of God would permit the same. By the law of God many persons be prohibited which be not expressed, but be understand by like prohibition in equal degree. Where it is there expressed that the nephew shall not marry his uncle's wife, it must needs be understand that the niece shall not be married unto the aunt's husband, because that all is one equality of degree. I trust this one reason shall satisfy all that be learned and of judgment. And as touching the Act of Parliament concerning the degrees prohibited by God's law, they be not so plainly set forth as I would they were. Wherein I somewhat spake my mind at the making of the said law, but it was not then accepted. I required them, that there must be expressed mother, and mother-in-law, daughter and daughter-in-law; and so in further 1 Jenkyns i. 20.

degrees directly upward and downward, in linea recta; also sister and sister-in-law, aunt and aunt-in-law, niece and niece-in-law. And this limitation, in my judgment, would have contained all degrees prohibited by God's law, expressed and not expressed, and should have satisfied this man, and such other which would marry their nieces-in-law." 1

Occasionally there is a little tiff between the friends. Cromwell thinks that Cranmer is not as quick as he might be over the divorce, and the Archbishop eagerly vindicates himself. 2 Another day, Cromwell is evidently in a very bad humour with him. He has charged him and his brother, the Archdeacon of Canterbury, with detaining property belonging to the King, and has written " very friendly " that he "would be sorry it should come to the King's knowledge." At the same time he had got Latimer to write to the Archbishop in his name to say that he "looked upon the King's business (of the Supremacy) through his fingers." " I marvel not," the Archbishop replies, " that you do so think, which knoweth not what I have done." 3 " I do not a little marvel," he says another time, " that you will think in me such lightness, to complain of one by whom I know no fault." 4 But it is not often that Cranmer writes with even so much of asperity. He knows the formidable countenance of the man with whom he is dealing. " If they once look you in the face," he writes, as he sends him a prisoner or two, "they shall have no power to conceal anything from you." 5 If he has a complaint to make, he makes it very gently. " Much business maketh

1 Jenkyns i. 173. Cranmer's rule was drawn out by Archbishop Parker, and became the law of the land under Elizabeth.

2 Jenkyns i. 25. 3 Ibid. i. 152. * Ibid. i. 146.

PUBLIC AFFAIRS UNDER HENRY 71

you to forget many things; and yet I wonder that you remember so many things as you do." 1 Sometimes there is a playful touch in the letters—occasionally a grim one. "I delivered unto you about Easter last passed a certain billet containing such matter as Friar Oliver preached in the last Lent"—in defence of the Pope—« which bill if ye had remembered, I doubt not but that ye would have provided for the same Friar afore this time; albeit there is no time yet lost, but that the same may be renewed again." 2 " If you could make Mr. Hutton an Abbot or Prior," he writes, in the year before the Six Articles, " and his wife an Abbess or a Prioress, he were most bound unto you. If you would help him to such a perfection, I dare undertake for him that he shall keep a better religion than was kept there before, though you appoint him unto the best house of religion in England." 3

It is curious how implicitly Cranmer believed that Cromwell—as he had believed that Ann Boleyn—was heart and soul labouring for the promotion of Cranmer's own Gospel. Again and again he claims his sympathetic interest in the cause. Now it is the spiritual darkness of Calais (then in the diocese of Canterbury) which distresses him: he pleads for the planting of " two learned persons" there who " shall shortly (no doubt) extirpate all manner of hypocrisy, false faith, and blindness of God and His word, wherein now the inhabitants there be altogether wrapt." 4 Now he begs that a living may be found for " Mr. Hambleton, put from his lands and possession in Scotland for that he favoureth the truth of God's word," "until it please.

1 Jenkyns i. 162. 2 Ibid. i. 120

God to send the true light of His gospel into his country." 1 Now he complains that the Bishop of Norwich " doth approve none to preach in his diocese that be of right judgment," and asks that certain grave men may have the King's license to preach there in spite of him, which would be " a deed very acceptable to God; for it were great pity that the diocese of Norwich should not be continued in the right knowledge of God which is begun amongst them." 2 Another time he sends him the names of certain men of Smarden and Pluckley in Kent, " indicted for unlawful assemblies at the last session at Canterbury, because they are accounted fautors of the new doctrine, as they call it," and asks protection for them. 3 Another time he urges a promotion for the father of the great Francis Bacon, on the ground that he is "of good judgment touching Christ's religion/' 4 It suited Cromwell to allow the Archbishop to believe in him; and indeed, like Northumberland in the reign of Edward VI., while in heart attached to the unreformed religion, if to any at all, he followed pretty steadily in action the policy of advancing the Reformation.

But as soon as the King's turn was served, the power of the Church broken, and the spoils of the monasteries gathered, Cromwell's knell rang. It was to no purpose that he acquiesced, or more than acquiesced, in the reaction of the Six Articles. There were stormy scenes between him and Henry. Sometimes the ferocious King would " bob him about the head " 6 in his anger. The miserable affair of Anne of Cleves brought matters to a point. Suddenly he fell; and the only voice in

1 Jenkyns i. 166, 184. 2 Ibid. i. 186. 3 Ibid. i. 243. 4 Ibid, i. 273. 5 See Dixon ii. 240, 241.

England that made itself heard on his behalf was that of the Archbishop of Canterbury. He, who had written to the enraged Sovereign on behalf of Ann Boleyn, now wrote to him an eloquent panegyric upon the doomed Cromwell.

" I heard yesterday in your Grace's Council that he is a traitor. Yet who cannot be sorrowful and amazed that he should be a traitor against your Majesty—he that was so advanced by your Majesty; he whose surety was only by your Majesty; he who loved your Majesty, as I ever thought, no less than God; he who studied always to set forwards what was your Majesty's will and pleasure; he that cared for no man's displeasure to serve your Majesty; he that was such a servant in my judgment, in wisdom, diligence, faithfulness, and experience, as no prince in this realm ever had; he that was so vigilant to preserve your Majesty from all treasons, that few could be so secretly conceived, but he detected the same in the beginning ? . . , I loved him as my friend, for so I took him to be; but I chiefly loved him for the love which I thought I saw him bear ever towards your Grace, singularly above all other." 1

Cromwell was beheaded six weeks after, on July 28, 1540; and the same day Henry married Catherine Howard, niece to the chief supporter of the party of the Old Learning.

There were, no doubt, many who supposed, either with hopes or with fears, that the Primate would have fallen along with the statesman to whom he clung. This was not to be the case. On the contrary, the removal of Cromwell from the scene only drew the King and the Archbishop more closely together. During the 1 Jenkyns i. 298.

seven years which remained of Henry's life, Cranmer transferred to the King the timid, affectionate confidence with which for the seven years past he had leant upon Cromwell. And the King, really fond of his simple and unworldly " chaplain," took a delight in watching and defeating the plots that were laid against him. " You," said Cromwell one day to the Archbishop, after the Archbishop had spoken out against the bill of the Six Articles, " you were born in a happy hour, I suppose; for do or say what you will, the King will always well take it at your hand. And I must needs confess, that in some things I have complained of you unto his Majesty, but all in vain, for he will never give credit against you, whatsoever is laid to your charge." 1 The first of the plots against Cranmer which followed the execution of Cromwell arose out of his own ecclesiastical family. His sense of fairness had led him, with the King's approval, to distribute his patronage in the reformed cathedral between the Old and the New Learning. The six preacherships were avowedly filled upon this principle; the twelve canonries were mostly filled by former monks. Series, one of the preachers, and Sandwich, one of the canons, were the most outspoken in opposing their patron, the Archbishop; and from the account given in Strype it would seem that the Archbishop did not always get the best of it. One Trinity Sunday the Archbishop summoned them all to Croydon and lectured them. He told Series, who had said in preaching that images in churches were not idols, that the two things were the same, only the one name was Latin and the other Greek. Sandwich, formerly a leading monk of Christ Church, and

1 Narratives of the Reformation p. 258.

Warden of Canterbury Hall at Oxford,1 had the hardihood to defend Series, and say " that he did not think so; an image, not abused with honour, is an image, and not an idol." It was a good defence; and the report got about in Canterbury that the Archbishop, unable to controvert it, had said that he "would be even with " Sandwich, and would make him " repent his reasoning with him." The meekest man sometimes loses patience with the rebels; and either then or another day Cranmer is said to have exclaimed—" You and your company hold me short; but I will hold you as short." War was now broken out. The malcontents of the Chapter allied themselves with the renowned visitor of monasteries, Dr. London, described by Archbishop Parker as " a stout and filthy Prebendary of Windsor," 2 who undertook the conduct of the business. Articles were carefully prepared in secret—first against Cranmer's chaplains, and then, as the spirits of the men rose, against the Primate himself. It was thought that he could be proved to have offended against the Act of the Six Articles. At length the indictment was introduced into the council-chamber, where Cranmer had many foes. Thence it passed into the King's hands. What followed must be told in the graphic language of Morice. " The King, on an evening, rowing on the Thames in his barge, came to Larnbeth Bridge, and there received my Lord Cranmer into his barge, saying unto him merrily—' Ah, my chaplain ! I have news for you ! I know now who is the greatest heretic in Kent.' And so pulled out of his sleeve a paper, wherein was contained his accusation, subscribed with the hands of

1 Jenkyns i. 238.

2 MSS. C.C.C.C, No. cxxviii. p. 203, as quoted by Strype.

certain prebendaries and justices of the shire. Where-unto my Lord Cranmer made answer, and besought his Highness to appoint such commissioners as would effectually try out the truth of those articles. ' Mary said the King, ' so will I do; for I have such affiance in your fidelity, that I will commit the examination hereof wholly unto you, and such as you will appoint.'" When the Archbishop objected that it would not look well, the King stuck to his point: Cranmer, he said, would tell him the truth, even unquestioned, if he had offended.

The Archbishop called the complainants before him, and expostulated with them. " 0 Mr. St. Leger," he exclaimed passionately, to one of the canons, " I had a good judgment in you; but ye will not leave your old mumpsimus." " I trust," retorted St. Leger, " we use no mumpsimuses but those that are consonant to the laws of God and the Prince." Others were less bold. One of them burst out weeping at the Archbishop's fatherly address. But it was a difficult matter to get to the bottom of; and the inquiry dragged on without much result, until Morice, the Archbishop's secretary, took it upon him to write to some of the Council, requesting to have some other commissioners despatched to his master's aid. He particularly asked for Dr. Leigh, who had had great experience in such investigations. Leigh in an instant sent men to search the houses of all the prebendaries and others who were thought to be mixed up in the matter. Letters were found which showed plainly that not only was Cranmer's favoured Suffragan, the Bishop of Dover, acquainted with all the proceedings, but the conspirators had throughout 1 Narratives of the Reformation p. 252.

received advice and encouragement from Gardiner, Bishop of Winchester. Then began confessions and entreaties. " Gentle father," wrote Sandwich to the Archbishop, " I have not borne so good, so tender a heart to you as a true child ought to bear. I ask of you mercy, with as contrite a heart as ever did David ask of God. And yet, good father, I did never bear malice against you. The greatest cause that ever occupied my heart against you was that I saw so little quietness among us, and so great jars in Christ's religion, supposing that by your permission and sufferance it did arise, which was not so, as I do now perceive. Good father, I have given myself unto you, heart, body, and service; and you have taken me unto you." To tears and prayers of this kind, Cranmer replied by casting up his hands to heaven, and thanking God that amidst so many enemies, he had one great friend and master, without whom he could not stand a day. He prayed God to make them good men; and added that there was no fidelity upon earth; he feared his left hand would accuse his right; but it was what Christ had prophesied of the latter days. He prayed God shortly to finish that time. A brief imprisonment followed, and such of the conspirators as were in the Archbishop's service were dismissed from their posts. 1

1 The account is given by Strype Cranmer vol. i. 244 foil. Bishop Gardiner, it must be owned, behaved with moderation and prudence. Visiting Canterbury one day, he asked Sandwich about the state of things there, who told him how little Kidley's and Scory's sermons agreed with those of the rest. Gardiner told him that he was sure Cranmer would look to it. He advised Sandwich never to preach without having his sermon in writing, and when any one else preached and he did not like it, " hold you contented and meddle not; so shall you do best." He did, however, say that Shether, instead of crying like a child, ought to have stood out against Cranmer.

Another time the accusation of Cranmer's heresies was made openly in Parliament, by a knight of the name of Gostwick, who had been a secretary of Cromwell's, 1 and held an official position. When the incident came to the King's ears, "his Highness marvellously stormed at the matter, and said that Gostwick had plied a villainous part so to abuse in open Parliament the Primate of the realm, specially being in favour with his Prince, as he was. ' What will they,' quod the King, ' do with him, if I were gone ?' Whereupon the King sent word unto Mr. Gostwick after this sort—' Tell that varlet Gostwick that if he do not acknowledge his fault unto my Lord of Canterbury, I will sure both make him a poor Gostwick, and otherwise punish him to the example of others.' " 2

A more formidable attempt to overthrow Archbishop Cranmer, on the part of the Lords in the Council attached to the Old Learning, has been made familiar to all Englishmen by the genius of Shakespeare— though Shakespeare, for dramatic reasons, has boldly placed it twelve years too early. Complaint was made to the King in person, that Cranmer and his learned men with their unsavoury doctrines, had made three parts of the land to become abominable heretics. England was thereby in danger of being divided against itself, like Germany. The Lords begged that he might be committed to the Tower, until he could be examined. Henry was not at all disposed to consent; but when it was represented that so long as Cranmer continued to be a member of Council no one would dare to give evidence against him, he agreed that he should be

1 See Index to Gasquet's Monasteries.
2 Narratives of the Reformation p. 254.

arrested next day if the Council then saw cause. That same night Cranmer was roused towards midnight by a messenger who summoned him to the King. The Archbishop rose, crossed from Lambeth to Whitehall, and found the King pacing in his gallery. Henry told him what had happened, and asked what he thought of the proposal of the Council. Cranmer thanked him humbly for the warning, and said that he would willingly go to the Tower until his doctrine was tried. " Oh Lord God exclaimed the King, " what fond simplicity have you, so to permit yourself to be imprisoned, that every enemy of yours may take vantage against you!" He would not hear of such a thing. He told him to go to the Council next day, and if the Council should insist on committing him to the Tower, to display to them a ring, which the King gave him, by which they would know that the King would have no one deal with the matter but himself.

The next morning he was summoned to the Council by eight o'clock; but when he arrived, entrance was denied him. Above three-quarters of an hour he was kept waiting outside the door, among servingmen and lacqueys, while many councillors and others passed in and out. Morice, the faithful secretary, indignant at the insult to his master, went to Dr. Butts, the King's physician. Dr. Butts came and saw with his eyes, and then went and told the King. " Have they served me so ?" cried Henry. " It is well enough; I shall talk with them by and by." At length Cranmer was called in. The ring was shown. Then Russell, the Lord President, swore a great oath, and said—"Did not I tell you, my Lords, what would come of this matter? I knew right well that the King would never permit my

Lord of Canterbury to have such a blemish as to be imprisoned, unless it were for high treason." Business was broken off, and they all went straight to the King. When they came near, Henry burst out—" Ah, my Lords! I had thought that I had a discreet and wise Council, but now I perceive that I am deceived. How have ye handled here my Lord of Canterbury ? What, make ye of him a slave, shutting him out of the Council chamber amongst serving men? Would ye be so handled yourselves ? I would you should well understand, that I account my Lord of Canterbury as faithful a man towards me as ever was prelate in this realm, and one to whom I am many ways beholding, by the faith I owe unto God "—here he laid his hand upon his breast —" and therefore whoso loveth me will regard him thereafter." Upon this speech, they all, and especially the Duke of Norfolk, offered an excuse. They meant no harm to the Archbishop by putting him in the Tower; they thought that after his trial he would be set at liberty to his greater glory. " Well," said Henry, " I pray you use not my friends so. I perceive now well enough how the world goeth among you. There remaineth malice among you one to another. Let it be avoided out of hand, I would advise you." " And so "the King departed," says Morice, "and the Lords shook hands every man with my Lord Cranmer, against whom nevermore after no man durst spurn during the King Henry's life." *

1 Narratives of the Reformation p. 254 foil.

CHAPTER III

CRANMER AND THE REFORMATION UNDER HENRY

IT was the fashion of those who were opposed to Cranmer in the earlier part of his episcopate, to speak of him as an ignorant man, of no education. An amusing story is told of one such calumniator, a Yorkshire priest, who, sitting among his neighbours at the alehouse, said that the Primate had " as much learning as the goslings of the green that go yonder." He was committed to prison by the Council, and lay there eight or nine weeks. When it came to Cranmer's knowledge, Cranmer sent for him, and invited him to " appose," or examine him, " in grammar, or else in philosophy and other sciences, or divinity." When the priest declined— " Well then," said my Lord, " I will appose you. Are you not wont to read the Bible ? " All clergymen were at this time ordered to do so. "Yes, that we do daily," the man replied. " I pray you, then," said Cranmer, " tell me who was David's father ?" The priest stood still, and said, " I cannot surely tell your Grace." Then said my Lord again, " If you cannot tell me, yet declare unto me, who was Solomon's father ?" " Surely," answered the priest, " I am nothing at all seen in those geneologies." " God amend ye," said the Archbishop, " and get ye home to your cure, and from henceforth learn to be an honest man, or at least a reasonable man." Cromwell came a few days later to see the Archbishop, and swore that the popish knaves should pick out Cranrner's eyes and cut his throat, before he would again rebuke them for slandering him. 1

As a matter of fact, Cranmer was one of the most learned men of his age, " At all times," says his secretary, "when the King's Majesty would be resolved in any doubt or question, he would but send word to my Lord overnight, and by the next day the King should have in writing brief notes of the Doctors' minds, as well divines as lawyers, both ancient, old, and new, with a conclusion of his own mind; which he could never get in such a readiness of none, no not of all his chaplains and clergy about him, in so short a time. For, being thoroughly seen in all kinds of expositors, he could incontinently lay open thirty, forty, sixty, or more somewhiles of authors, and so, reducing the notes of them all together, would advertise the King more in one day, than all his learned men could do in a month. And it was no marvel; for it was well known that commonly, if he had not business of the Prince's, or special urgent causes before him, he spent three parts of the day in study as effectually as [if] he had been at Cambridge. And therefore it was that the King said on a time to the Bishop of Winchester (the King and my said Lord of Winchester defending together that the 1 Canons of the Apostles' were of as good authority as the four Evangelists, contrary to my Lord Cranmer's assertion),' My Lord of Canterbury said the King, ' is too old a Trewante for us twain.'" 2

1 Narratives of the Reformation p. 269 foil.

2 Ibid. p. 249. The word Trewante is explained to mean

THE REFORMATION UNDER HENRY 83

When Bishop Ridley, himself a man of great attainments, was a prisoner in the Tower, Queen Mary's secretary, Bourne, hinted to him that Cranmer's book on the Eucharist was not really Cranmer's, but his. " ' Mr. Secretary,' quoth I"—it is Ridley who tells the tale— "' that book was written of a great learned man, and him which is able to do the like again. As for me, I ensure you (be not deceived in me), I was never able to do or write any such like thing. He passeth me no less than the learned master his young scholar " 1

Some idea of the range of Archbishop Cranmer's learning may be formed by examining the list of his remaining books, which has been made by Mr. Edward Burbidge. 2 That list includes some 350 printed volumes, and about 100 manuscripts. Of course, this number represents but a small fraction of the Archbishop's library, of which, no doubt, most is now lost or destroyed. It is, as Mr. Burbidge says, " nothing less than astonishing " to find the traces of so wide and deep a study of Scripture in those days. There are two Hebrew Bibles of Cranmer's in existence, besides the great Complutensian Polyglott, together with Kimchi's Hebrew and Latin Commentary on the earlier Psalms, and three works on the Hebrew language. One of the Hebrew Bibles is interleaved with a Latin translation of Cranmer's own, in Cranmer's hand. It is needless to say, after that, though the fact was formerly questioned, that the Archbishop was familiar with Greek. Morice's statement about his master's knowledge of expositors

Trojan, i. e. a fighter; but perhaps it is only truant, used in a general familiar way, as "beggar," "knave" (see Skeat s. v. Truant), l Quoted in Jenkyns i. lxxxv.

of the Bible is well borne out by the evidence. Not only do we still find in different places an almost complete set of the Latin and Greek Fathers—several of them in various editions—as well as an imposing array of the works of the Schoolmen—the Angelic and the Seraphic, the Subtle, the Irrefragable, the Invincible, and all the rest:—his direct Commentaries upon Holy Scripture include the great exegetical works of Thomas Aquinas (in edition after edition), of Denys the Carthusian, of Euthymius and Œcumenius, and other "old" authors. The "new" of every school are well represented by Bucer and Cajetan, by Erasmus and his adversary Faber, by Francis Titelmann and Melan-chthon. Of Cranmer's books on Liturgiology and other subjects, it is only necessary here to say that we have proof of an immense and highly diversified erudition.

That Archbishop Cranmer was well acquainted with the books which he thus amassed is proved not only by the frequent annotations in his own hand which enrich them;—Mr. Burbidge justly calls especial attention to his copies of Eusebius and of Epiphanius ;—the same is shown by his manuscript Commonplace Books. Of these several exist, of greater or less extent. 1 The history of the most important of them is in part known. That famous antiquary Archbishop Parker," with spying and searching," discovered it to be in the hands of a certain Dr. Nevison, Canon of Canterbury, who, having no right to it, denied that he had it. Thereupon Parker wrote to ask the help of the Council in

[1] The Lambeth Library contains a Collection of Laws, showing the extravagant pretensions of Rome (Stillingiieet, 1107), and Notes on Justification (Stillingfleet, 1108). These are printed in Jenkyns ii. 1 and 121.

THE REFORMATION UNDER HENRY 85

recovering the books, saying that he would "as much rejoice to win them, as to restore an old chancel to reparation." Sir William Cecil, who in early days had presumed to admonish Cranmer for his faults,[1] now rejoiced to hear " of such hid treasures as he took the books of the holy Archbishop Cranmer to be." He had himself lately recovered five or six written books of his. Letters from the Council were soon despatched to Archbishop Parker, authorising him to search the canon's house; and the prize is now in the British Museum, with this correspondence prefixed to it.[2]

The work, which has never been printed, is in two large folio volumes, written mainly in Ralph Morice's hand, partly also in those of other secretaries. It has evidently been put together at different epochs in Cranmer's life; and an accurate study of it would help to show the gradual formation of its author's opinion upon many of the points of which it treats. It contains an immense number of extracts—from Clement of Rome and Ignatius; from Irenaeus and Tertullian, Origen and Cyprian; Lactantius, Hilary, Ambrose, Paulinus of JNola, Augustine, Fulgentius, Jerome, Vincent of Lerins, Cas-sian, Prudentius, Gelasius, Leo, Sulpicius Severus, Gregory the Great, and Bede; from Eusebius, Epipha-nius, Athanasius, Basil, Gregory of Nazianzus, Chry-sostom, Cyril of Alexandria, Socrates and Sozomen, Theophilus of Alexandria, Denys the Areopagite, John Damascene, Nicephorus Chartophylax; from Ra-banus arid Haymo, Aldhelm, Bruno, Bernard, Anselm,

[1] Jenkyns i. 351.

[2] 7 B. xi. xii. The letters are printed in Archbishop Parker's Correspondence pp. 186—195.

Dagobert, Otto of Freising; from Peter Lombard, Thomas Aquinas, Duns Scotus, Hugh of St. Victor, Albert the Great, Alexander of Hales; from the letters of the Popes (real and forged); from the Canons of Councils, ecumenical and provincial, foreign and English, down to the Capitulum Coloniense; from the Ordinary Gloss and Lyranus; from Durandus and Honorius de Celebratione Missarum, Paulus Cortosius and Panor-mitanus, Orbellensis and Gerson, Stapulensis, Erasmus, Bilibald Pirckheimer, Eckius, Cajetanus, Luther, Oeco-lampadius, Osiander, Bucer, Brentius, Melanchthon, Calvin, Bullinger; and many others.

Sometimes the extracts are interrupted to give the rdsumd of an argument of Eckius or Calvin, sometimes objections or reasonings of Cranmer's own. He weighs the consequences of accepting universal traditions, and how the Pope's position would or would not be thereby strengthened.[1]

[1] The extracts have been made on sheets of paper, which have been stitched together afterwards. Evidently the present form is not the earliest form, because, although the hands vary, no one section is, so far as I have seen, by more than one hand. The extracts from the Greek writers are given in a Latin version. Here and there, the arguments and reasonings are in English. So far as I have been able to observe, there are no extracts from Gregory of Nyssa (though the Archbishop had at any rate one of his works ; see Burbidge xxiL), nor from Clement of Alexandria, Didymus, or Cyril of Jerusalem. It is more noteworthy that there are none from Isidore of Seville or Amalarius, though he possessed MSS. of some of their writings ; see Burbidge xvii. xix. Subjoined is the list of contents, written (unless I mistake) in Morice's hand, though the paging (which I have not given) was not completed by him, and has only been filled

in with pencil.

Tabula Repertoria.

1. Sacre scripturae intellectus et vtilitas.
2. Quod Authorum scripta, sine verbo dei, non sunt accipienda pro articulis fidei.

THE REFORMATION UNDER HENRY 87

There is no distinguishable point of time at which Thomas Cranmer began to take the reforming side in

3. Scripturse confirmantes idem.
4. Doctores idem probantes.
5. Kaciones in idem.
6. Conciliorum decreta sine scriptura, non stint accipienda pro articulis fidei.
7. Veteres Canones Abrogati.
8. Ex Angelorum oraculis non licet idem facere.
9. Nee miraculis idem probare phas est.
10. Nee eciam Apparitio mortuorum idipsum satis Astruit.
11. Sed iiec consuetudini, hac in re fidendum est.
12. Obiectiones, quod prseter scripturae Authoritatem, accipiendi sunt noui articuli fidei.
13. Tradiciones non scriptae.
14. Raciones in idem.
15. Nee miracula, nee Christi professio, nee locus, nee externtim aliquod, faciunt honiinem sanctum, aut deo gratum, sed observacio mandatorum dei.
16. Noue doctrinae.
17. In Cerimoniis fere omnibus, ludeos imitamur.
18. Osiander.
19. De sacrifices Christianorum.
20. De sacramentis.
21. De charactere.
22. De baptismo.
23. De Eucharistia.
24. De paeniteneia. *De confessione.
25. De Satisfactione.
26. De Matrimonio.
27. De ordinibus ecclesiasticis.
28. De Vnctione.
29. De Impositione manuum.
30. De Confirmacione.
31. De extrema vnctione.
32. De vnctione paedum [for De locione pedum].
33. De Aqua benedicta.
34. De feriis.
35. De Sanctorum Invocacione.
36. De Imaginibus.
37. De diuorum Reliquiis

38. De vera Religione et supersticione.
39. Vt oremus, aut peccatorum veniam consequamur, non est
vllus locus prae alio deo acceptior, nee pro hiis opus est longe pegrinari.

the controversies of the age. It appears that from the Cambridge days of Erasmus he was in sympathy with those who, in the language of the time, " favoured the Gospel." These men, of whom Bilney, Latimer, and Barnes were the chief, were not doctrinally at issue with the established religion. If they were accounted heretics, and were sometimes found abjuring their heresies, and sometimes burning for them, it was because of their unsparing denuntiation of practical abuses which had been sanctioned by time and by authority. Pilgrimages, the worship of images, indulgences (or "the Bishop of Rome's pardons," as they were called), the narrowness and presumption of the scholastic divinity, compulsory celibacy of the priest-

40. De Religiosis.
41. De votis.
42. De virginitate, et voto castitatis.
43. De Ecclesia.
44. De Ecclesiis edificandis, dedicandis, et earum ornatu.
45. De horis Canonicis.
46. De Oracione, et cantu Ecclesiastico.
47. De Ieiunio.
48. De ^lemosina.
49. De corruptis ecclesiae moribus.
50. De Excommunicacione.
51. De sepultura inortuorum.
52. De nrissa.
53. De diuinis proeceptis. *De Purgatorio.
54. De Gracia et meritis. *Contra Purgatorium.
55. De Libero Arbitrio.
56. Semper orandus est deus, yt condonet peccata, eciam piis
filiis, quibus iam omnia peccata dimissa sunt.
57. De beatissima virgine. *De conuersione impii.
58. De Obediencia erga magistratus. *Gracia prsecedit
meritum.
*De operibus ante spiritum sanctum. *De fide. *Contra merita humana.
* Added in later hand.

hood, the secular pomp of the higher clergy, superstitions of various kinds, were the object of their attacks. What they mainly desired was a freer and more spiritual Christianity than they found. One great practical reform which Cranmer had long desired to promote has already been mentioned—the liberation of his country from the yoke of Rome. Another was the diffusion of the Bible in English.

Archbishop Cranmer was, of course, far from being the first English Churchman who had laboured for this cause. Not to speak of earlier and more partial efforts, the great work of Wiclif had never been forgotten. It had drawn forth such a passionate love of the Bible in the hearts of Englishmen, that when Henry VIII/s commissioners of 1530, in Archbishop Warham's time, attempted to suppress the New Testament of Tyndale— mainly because of its venomous notes— and reported that no such translation was necessary, they yet felt constrained to add that if the English people showed signs of forsaking erroneous opinions, the King "intended to provide that the Holy Scriptures should be by great learned and Catholic persons translated into the English tongue, if it should then seem to his Grace convenient to do." 1 The matter did not interest Henry, but Cranmer took it up. In the first Convocation over which he presided, in 1534, the clergy joined to a request that heretical books might be called in, and that laymen should be restrained from public disputations on the faith, the request that his Majesty would nominate trustworthy persons to translate the sacred Scripture into the vulgar tongue, and permit the same to be delivered to the people according to their learning. 1 Dixon i. 42.

No royal action was taken upon this petition, but the zealous Primate himself endeavoured to form a committee for the purpose. Taking one of the existing versions of the New Testament, he divided it among the most learned of the bishops and others to be corrected and returned to him at a given date. Gardiner did the Gospels of St. Luke and St. John; he informs Cromwell, in June 1535, that he has finished them. 1 Stokesley was to have done the Acts of the Apostles; but when Cranmer sent his secretary to Fulham to ask for the book, the Bishop only replied that he "marvelled what my Lord of Canterbury meant;" it was " abusing the people to give them liberty to read the Scriptures, and did nothing else but infect them with heresies. I have bestowed never an hour upon my portion," he said, " nor never will." On the secretary's return to Lambeth Cranmer marvelled at the Bishop's froward-ness, that he would not do as other men did; but a wag who was present explained, to the Archbishop's amusement, that our Lord had left nothing in His "Testament " to Bishop Stokesley, and that the Apostles were "simple poor fellows," in whose acts the haughty prelate could not be expected to take an interest. 2

Reluctance on the part of some of those to whom the task was assigned was joined to cross-action on the part of the Vicegerent. Before Cranmer's committee-men could finish their work, Coverdale's version of the Bible appeared—the first printed version of the whole Bible in English. Cromwell drew up an Injunction in 1536, that by the middle of next year every parson should provide his church with a Latin Bible and an English,

1 See Jenkyns i. xxvii.
2 Narratives of the Reformation p. 277.

which could be no other than Coverdale's. The Injunction appears to have had for its sole effect the quashing of Cranmer's project, for Coverdale's Bible never came into the churches. 1 But the year after, when "Matthew's" Bible was issued, Cranmer was much pleased with it—indeed, he is thought to have been cognisant beforehand of its preparation. 2 He sent a copy of it to Cromwell, with the request that it might be licensed " until such time that we, the Bishops, shall set forth a better translation, which I think," he pursues, " will not be till a day after doomsday. And if you continue to take such pains for the setting forth of God's word as you do, although in the mean season you surfer some snubs, and many slanders, lies, and reproaches for the same, yet one day He will requite altogether. And the same word (as St. John saith) which shall judge every man at the last day, must needs show favour to them that now do favour it 3 Although Matthew's Bible was disfigured by many of the same features which had disfigured Tyndale's New Testament, the petition of Cranmer was granted. Nine days later he writes a glowing letter of thanks. " You have shewed me more pleasure herein than if you had given me a thousand pound. Hereby such fruit of good knowledge shall ensue, that it shall well appear hereafter, what high and acceptable service you have done unto God and the King, which shall so much redound to your honour, that, besides God's reward, you shall obtain perpetual memory for the same within the realm. And, as for me, you may reckon me your bondman for the same." 4

The Archbishop's overflowing

1 Dixon i. 447. 2 Westcott English Bible p. 70.

delight could not rest without writing again a fortnight after. " These shall be to give you most hearty thanks that any heart can think, and that in the name of them all which favoureth God's word. This deed you shall hear of at the great day, when all things shall be opened and made manifest." 1

A new and more wholesome edition of this book was prepared at Paris in 1538 by Coverdale—curiously enough under the supervision of the famous Bonner, who, on his promotion directly after to the see of London, set up six copies in the nave of St. Paul's. This edition was partly destroyed by the French Inquisition, but was finally completed in England, where it was introduced by a new Injunction of the Vicegerent, to the effect that every parish church was to have " one book of the whole Bible of the largest volume/' and the parishioners to be "provoked to read the same." Archbishop Cranmer wrote for this—the " Great Bible," as it is called—a Preface, which is one of his most felicitous pieces of work. Some there were, he said, that were too slow, and needed the spur; some other too quick, and needed more of the bridle. Some lost their game by short shooting; some by overshooting. Of the one sort were those who refused to read or listen to the Scriptures; of the other, those whose conduct hindered the word of God which they professed to further. Although the Scriptures are light, and food, and fire, Cranmer did not wonder that, at their first introduction, men who have been accustomed to live without them should fail to appreciate them, as savages who have lived on mast and acorns objected to bread made of good corn. And yet, in the Archbishop's opinion, 1 Jenkyns i. 200.

THE REFORMATION UNDER HENRY 93

the reading of the Bible was no novelty in England. "It is not much above one hundred years ago since Scripture hath not been accustomed to be read in the vulgar tongue within this realm: and many hundred years before that, it was translated and read in the Saxons' tongue, which at that time was our mother's tongue; whereof there remaineth yet divers copies, found lately in old abbeys, of such antique manners of writing and speaking that few men now been able to read and understand them. 1 And when this language waxed old and out of common usage, because folk should not lack the fruit of reading, it was again translated into the newer language, whereof yet also many copies remain, and be daily found." A long and spirited translation from St. Chrysostom deals with the cavillers of Bishop Stokesley's type, and ends—" The reading of Scriptures is a great and strong bulwark or fortress against sin; the ignorance of the same is the greater ruin and destruction of them that will not know it. That is the thing that bringeth in heresy; that is it that causeth all corrupt and perverse living; that is it that bringeth all things out of good order." As St. Chrysostom was invoked to reprove those who refused to read the Bible, so St. Gregory of Nazianzus is brought in to reprove the other sort of offenders. " It appeareth that in his time there were some (as I fear me there been also now at these days a great number) which were idle babblers and talkers of the Scripture out of season and all good order, and without any increase of virtue, or example of good living. To them he writeth all his first book, De Theologia," of which Cranmer proceeds to

1 A MS. of the four Gospels in Anglo-Saxon, which belonged to Cranmer, is preserved in the British Museum (1 A. xiv.).

give a vigorous summary. It is not fit for every man to dispute the high questions of divinity. It is dangerous for the unclean to touch that thing that is most clean; like as the sore eye taketh harm by looking upon the sun, Contention and debate about Scriptures doth most hurt to ourselves and to the cause that we would have furthered. " All our holiness consisteth in talking;

and we pardon each other from all good living, so that we may stick fast together in argumentation." To conclude, says the Archbishop in his own words, "every man that cometh to the reading of this holy Book ought to bring with him first and foremost the fear of Almighty God; and then next, a firm and stable purpose to reform his own self according thereunto, and so to continue, shewing himself to be a sober and fruitful hearer and learner," lest he lay himself open to the challenge of the Psalm, " Why dost thou preach My laws, and takest My testament in thy mouth, whereas thou hatest to be reformed, and hast been partaker with advoutrers ?" 1

In 1542, after the fall of Cromwell, a fresh effort was made. The Great Bible failed to give satisfaction—at any rate to the clergy of the Old Learning, now in the ascendant. Convocation declared, in reply to a question of the Archbishop, that it could not be without scandal retained, unless it were revised. A revision was agreed upon. The Bible was partitioned among groups of scholars and prelates. Bishop Gardiner signalised himself on this occasion by naming a curious list of Latin words which he thought it important to use in the English translation of the Bible; but other-

1 The Preface is printed in Jenkyns ii. 104 foil. It only appears in the later editions of the Great Bible.

wise he does not seem to have been opposed to the project any more than to that of seven years before. Suddenly, however, the work was stopped by royal orders. The King, so Cranmer announced, had determined to commit the translation to the two Universities. It is affirmed^ and reaffirmed by serious authors, that this was a ruse of Cramner's, who was afraid lest Gardiner should carry his point. 1 Of this there is no evidence whatever—it is only a surmise of Strype's; but to the angry remonstrances of Convocation Cranmer replied that he should abide by the King's decision. If indeed the King's decision was due to Cranmer's own suggestion, Cranmer's behaviour in the matter is inexplicable. The Universities received no communication upon the subject from the King, and there was no further attempt to provide an authoritative translation while Henry lived.

The general English public in Henry VIII.'s reign was but little acquainted with the progress of events upon the Continent of Europe; and our Reformation, before the accession of Edward VI,, was not much affected by the divines of Germany and Switzerland. Cranmer, who had travelled in Germany, and had married a German wife, was one of the few Englishmen who kept up an intercourse with foreign scholars. Although by no mean's disposed—at least in those days— to make the English Church a humble pupil of Wittenberg or of Zurich, he wished to see co-operation and a good intelligence between the reforming party abroad and his own emancipated Church. The Protestant princes of Germany had formed a league for mutual defence, and negotiations passed between them and 1 See for instance Westcott English Bible 113.

Henry on the subject of his joining it. In 1535 Henry sent to Schmalcalden, where the league assembled, an embassy headed by his former almoner Edward Foxe, recently made Bishop of Hereford. To him was joined one of those men of secondary importance in history, whose careers display in the most instructive manner the shifting currents of an age of transition. This was Nicholas Heath, destined in Mary's reign to become Archbishop of York and Lord High Chancellor, in which capacity he signed the death-warrant of Cranmer. Heath was at this time all on the side of progress. He is said to have spoken boldly to Cranmer in defence of Frith's doctrine of the Eucharist, when Cranmer still thought it "notably erroneous." 1 The Archbishop, always unstinting in his praise of those who were upon his side, commended him to Cromwell as one "which for his learning, wisdom, discretion, and sincere mind toward his prince, I know no man in my judgment more meet to serve the King's Highness' purpose "; and he urged that he should be provided with a stipend fit for an ambassador. 2 The Archdeaconry of Stafford was assigned to him as an endowment, as that of Taunton had been assigned to Cranmer for a similar purpose; and he held that preferment when, with Foxe and ^Barnes, he attended the gathering at Schmalcalden. Kot much was gained at that gathering, either in the waV of doctrinal agreement or in bringing the Ger-mams to commit themselves to the King's divorce ; but

1 R)xe viii. 699 (ed. 1849).

2 Jetikyns i. 87. It is doubtful whether this letter refers to the Sciimalcalden mission, or whether Heath had already been sent intip Germany. The mention of "the King's great cause" alone, irftay be thought to show that it belongs to a somewhat earlier tinne.

Cranmer's opinion of Heath was justified by the irn-pression which he made upon Melanchthon. " The Archdeacon, Nicholas Heath," wrote Melanchthon to Camerarius, "is the only one of our guests who is distinguished by culture and learning; the rest are destitute of our philosophy and sweetness, so I avoid their society as much as I can." l The German princes offered to make Henry the Defender of their league on condition of his accepting the Confession of Augsburg* This the old antagonist of Luther declined to do. Bishop Gardiner supplied him with cogent political reasons for declining; and it is probable that Archbishop Cranmer, if he was consulted, would support the decision by theological arguments.

It was now judged advisable that the English Church, which, by the lips of the Supreme Head, had several times, since the breach with Rome, declared that she had no intention of varying in any point from the true Catholic faith, should express in some detail what that faith, in her judgment, was. German divines were to see how far the English were prepared to go along with them. Diversities at home would be rallied to an authoritative standard. Accordingly, in 1536, the Ten Articles were prepared, the first precursors of our present Thirty-Nine. They bore the title of Articles devised ly the King's Highness* Majesty, to stablish Christian quietness and unity among us, and to avoid contentious opinions: which Articles ~be also approved by the consent and determination of the whole clergy of this realm. Whose hand drew them up cannot now be ascertained, but the first signature to them, after the Vicar General's,

1 Seckendorf Gomm. de Luth. lib. iii. § xxxix. Add. (e.), quoted by Jenkyns i. 87.

is naturally that of Cranmer; and they well represent his state of opinion at the time. These Articles, as the preface states, are divided into two parts—a division which lays the true basis of our Catholic Reformation, and which Cranmer rightly claims as a great re-discovery of the time. 1 "The one part containeth such [Articles] as be commanded expressly by God, and be necessary to our salvation ; and the other containeth such things as have been of a long continuance for a decent order and honest policy prudently instituted and used in the churches of our realm, although they be not expressly commanded of God, nor necessary to our salvation." Acceptance of the canonical Scriptures, and of the three Creeds, as the rule of faith; holy Baptism; the sacrament of Penance, as a necessity for all who have committed mortal sin after baptism, but explained after a truly evangelical manner; the presence of Christ's Body and Blood in the Eucharist briefly stated, though without using the technical terms of transubstantiation; Justification, defined in the words of Melanchthon, and to be attained by contrition and faith, joined with charity, but not as though these were its meritorious cause ; these are the first necessary part of the little book. In the second part the people are taught how to use and how not to use sacred images, how to honour and how not to honour saints, what kind of prayers may be addressed to saints, the meaning of various rites and ceremonies which are instructive and laudaJble, though they have no power to remit sin; and of Purgatory, that no man ought to be grieved at the continuance of prayers for the departed, " that they may b^ relieved and holpen of some part of their 1 Jenkyns i. 216.

pain," l but that " the place where they be, the name thereof, and kind of pains there, be to us uncertain by Scripture," so that the abuses connected with the doctrine ought to be clearly put away, such as that " the Bishop of Rome's pardons," or masses said at Scala Cadi or otherwhere, could send souls straight to heaven. 2

These Articles were put forth in July 1586. In the preface to them, the King declared that if they were obediently received by the people, he should be not a little encouraged " to take further travails, pains, and labours " for their commodities. There was, indeed, much left to be desired in the reception of the Articles and of the royal Injunctions which accompanied them. At the time of their appearance, the abbeys were fast falling, and the " Pilgrimage of Grace" attested the unpopularity of the King's measures. The northern clergy assembled and passed a series of reactionary resolutions. Henry turned fiercely upon the bishops of the reforming school, and, probably more to appease the opposite faction than for any other reason, upbraided them in a general manifesto for speaking against accustomed ceremonies in spite of the Ten Articles and Injunctions.

Nevertheless, he was so well pleased with his first attempt at doctrinal pacification, that a further step was determined upon. At the beginning of the next year, Cromwell summoned the bishops to a meeting. After he had opened the proceedings, the Archbishop of Canterbury thus stated the business in hand—

1 In the original draft, it seems to have run, "that they may sooner obtain the mercy of God and fruition of His glory." The alteration is probably due to the King's own hand.

2 The Ten Articles, together with the Bishops' Book and the King's Book, may be found in Lloyd's Formularies of Faith put forth by Authority in the reign of Henry VIII. (Oxford, 1856).

" There be weighty controversies now moved and put forth, not of ceremonies and light things, but of the true understanding and of the right difference of the Law and the Gospel; of the manner and way how sins be forgiven; of comforting doubtful and wavering consciences, by what means they may be certified that they please God, seeing they feel the strength of the law accusing them of sin ; of the true use of the Sacraments, whether the outward work of them doth justify man, or whether we receive our justification by faith. Item, which be the good works, and the true service and honour which pleaseth God ; and whether the choice of meats, the difference of garments, the vows of monks and priests, and other traditions which have no word of God to confirm them, whether these, I say, be right good works, and such as make a perfect Christian man, or no. Item, whether vain service and false honouring of God, and man's traditions, do bind men's consciences, or no. Finally, whether the ceremony of Confirmation, of Orders, and of Annealing, and such other, which cannot be proved to be institute of Christ, nor have any word in them to certify us of remission of sins, ought to be called Sacraments, and to be compared with Baptism and the Supper of the Lord, or no."

"Unfortunately for the cause of peace, Cromwell had introduced into the meeting the Scotchman Aless, who was at this time a guest of the Archbishop's at Lambeth. Aless had sojourned long among the Lutherans of Germany, and delivered himself with an assurance which provoked the deep resentment of Bishop Stokesley and other prelates of the Old Learning. Yet so loyal were they all to the cause of Catholic unity, that there was 1 Jenkyns ii. 16.

no difficulty in forming a committee, by whose labours in a very short time was produced the Institution of a Christian Man, commonly known as the Bishops* Book. In this work, Cranmer, along with Bishop Foxe, had the chief share. 1 No small amount of discretion and conciliatory feeling must have been required to bring such diversity of views into agreement. It is impossible without emotion to read this grave and fervent, practical and large-minded, exposition of the Christian faith and life, as understood by the Church of England under Henry, and to see the names appended to it. Side by side with Archbishop Cranmer's, appears the name of Edward Lee of York, the old antagonist of Erasmus. Stokesley and Gardiner, Tunstall, Clerk, Veysey, Long-land, and Sampson, are willing to be considered its joint authors with Latimer and Shaxton, Goodrich, Foxe, Hillsey, and Barlow. Among the signatures of men who were not yet bishops, stand those of Bonner, Skip, and Heath, of Richard Smith, and May, Nicholas Wot ton, and Richard Cox. He would have been a bold man who would have undertaken in 1537 to say in what directions this united band of divines would afterwards diverge.

The " Bishops' Book " contained an explanation of the Creed, the Seven Sacraments, the Ten Commandments, the Pater Noster, and the Ave Maria; of Justification, and of Purgatory. Doctrinally, it occupies the same position as the Ten Articles, upon which it is founded. On some of the crucial points, such as Penance and the Eucharist, Justification and Purgatory, it only repeats the Articles with a few verbal alterations. Although all the seven Sacraments are affirmed to deserve that 1 Latimer to Cromwell, in Jenkyns i. 188.

name, the Sacraments of Baptism, Penance, and of the Altar are set above the rest, as having been instituted by Christ Himself with outward visible signs and conveying graces whereby sins are remitted. The Ave Maria is explained to be not a prayer, but an act of praise only, and nothing is said about the invocation of her or of other saints. The Church of Rome is to be considered as only one Church among many.

There is one doctrine dealt with in the " Bishops' Book," of which it is necessary to take more extended notice, because about this time Cranmer's personal opinion on it was inclined to vary from what he acknowledged as binding in public. It is the doctrine of Holy Orders, and of ecclesiastical authority. Towards the end of 1540, questions were sent round to all the bishops, with a view (as it seems) to the compilation of the " King's Book," which in 1542 superseded the " Bishops' Book." The questions were probably drawn up by Cranmer himself, and his answers to them remain, as well as those of other bishops. In these he states his opinion as follows—

"All Christian princes have committed unto them immediately of God the whole cure of all their subjects, as well concerning the administration of God's word for the cure of souls, as concerning the ministration of things political and civil governance : and in both these ministrations they must have sundry ministers under them to supply that which is appointed to their several offices. The civil ministers under his Majesty ... be those whom it shall please his Highness for the time to put in authority under him, as for example, the Lord Chancellor, Lord Treasurer, etc. The ministers of God's word under his Majesty be the bishops, parsons, vicars, and such other priests as be appointed by his Highness to that ministration : as for example, the Bishop of Canterbury . . . the Parson of Winwick, etc. All the said officers and ministers, as well of the one sort as of the other, be appointed, assigned, and elected in every place, by the laws and orders of kings and princes.

" In the admission of many of these officers be divers comely ceremonies and solemnities used, which be not of necessity, but only for a good order and seemly fashion; for if such offices and ministrations were committed without such solemnity, they were nevertheless truly committed. And there is no more promise of God that grace is given in the committing of the ecclesiastical office, than it is in the committing of the civil office."

In the Apostles' time, Cranmer continues, because there were no Christian princes to govern the Church, ministers could only be appointed by the consent of the Christian multitude among themselves. They took such curates and priests as they knew to be meet, or as were commended to them by men replete with the Spirit. Sometimes the Apostles appointed them; in which case the people with thanks accepted them, "not for the supremity, impery, or dominion, that the Apostles had over them to command, as their princes and masters, but as good people, ready to obey the advice of good counsellors."

Bishops and priests were "both one office in the beginning of Christ's religion. A bishop may make a priest by the Scripture, and so may princes and governors also, and that by the authority of God committed to them, and the people also by their election; for as we read that bishops have done it, so Christian emperors and princes usually have done it, and the people, before Christian princes were, commonly did elect their bishops and priests.

" In the New Testament, he that is appointed to be a bishop, or a priest, needeth no consecration by the Scripture, for election or appointing thereunto is sufficient."

To the question whether, by the Scripture, a bishop or priest may excommunicate, and whether they alone, the Archbishop replies that Scripture neither commands nor forbids them. If the law of the land permits them, they may; if it forbids, they may not; and the law may empower men who are not priests to excommunicate.

"This," writes Cranmer, at the end of his answers, " is mine opinion and sentence at this present; which, nevertheless, I do not temerariously define, but refer the judgment thereof wholly unto your Majesty."

Cranmer's opinion on the subject is of some controversial importance at the present time, inasmuch as his opinion was shared by some other prelates—notably by Bishop Barlow, the chief consecrator of Archbishop Parker. If the defective intention of Barlow was enough to invalidate his consecration of Parker, the same might with some justice be said of the twenty-three bishops consecrated by Archbishop Cranmer, which would introduce grave confusion into the history of the Church. But, as a matter of fact, neither Barlow nor Cranmer had the smallest wavering of intention with regard to the consecrations which they were performing. To fancy that the bishops whom they consecrated might have been as true bishops by the King's command, or the people's choice, without any of the " comely cere-1 See Jenkyns ii. 98 foil.

THE REFORMATION UNDER HENRY 105

monies and solemnities" in use, gives no proof of an inadequate intention or a failure of faith, when the due forms were actually employed. There was no contradiction between Cranmer's answers to the questions of 1540, and the full statement upon the Sacrament of Orders to which he had set his hand in the "Bishops' Book." The chapter on the Sacrament of Orders is the longest in that book. It unhesitatingly affirms that this Sacrament was " instituted by Christ and His Apostles in the New Testament;" that it has for its visible and outward sign " prayer and imposition of the bishop's hands ;" 1 that it has " annexed unto it assured promises of excellent and inestimable things ; " that" God hath instituted and ordained none other ordinary mean whereby He will make us partakers of the reconciliation which is by Christ, and confer and give the graces of His Holy Spirit unto us," except the Word and Sacraments, for the dispensing of which the ministry is necessary. Nor were these views only the prevalent views, acquiesced in by Cranmer for the sake of unity. When in 1548 he translated the Catechism of Justus Jonas, he put forth in his own name a statement concerning the sacred ministry which suggests no ambiguity. " The Apostles," it says, " laid their hands upon [others] and gave them the Holy Ghost, as they themselves received of Christ the same Holy Ghost, to execute this office. And they that were so ordained were indeed the ministers of God as the Apostles themselves were. Arid so the ministration of God's word (which our Lord Jesus Christ Himself did first institute) was derived from the Apostles unto others after them, by imposition of hands

1 It is noticeable that nothing is said of the porrection of the instruments.

and giving the Holy Ghost, from the Apostles' time to our days. And this shall continue in the Church, even to the world's end." 1

The " Bishops' Book " marks the point which had been reached by the reforming movement in 1537. It satisfied the respectable school of Reformers like Latimer; it carried along with it the conservatives like Tunstall. But it received no collective sanction from the Church; and the King, although he so far approved of it as to send it to the King of Scotland as an example for the Scotch to imitate, refused to give it his royal authority. 2

Cranmer himself is partly responsible for not having let well alone. He was anxious, like Cromwell, to resume the interrupted negotiations with the German Protestants. In May, 1538, a deputation from them arrived in England. It consisted of Burckhardt, Vice-chancellor of Saxony, and two others. They had hardly been a month in England before they endeavoured to gain from Cranmer a commutation of penance for a clergyman named Atkinson, who held novel opinions

1 Catechismus p. 196 (Oxford, 1829).

2 The King's strictures upon the " Bishops' Book " may be seen in Jenkyns ii. 21 foil., and on p. 65 foil. Cranmer's comments upon these strictures. For those who suppose that Cranmer's attitude was one of unvarying subserviency towards the royal theologian, it will be a good corrective to read his comments upon Henry's observations. The tone of them is strangely outspoken and free, as he criticises alike the grammar, the logic, and the theology of Henry. " I trust the King's Highness will pardon my presumption," he writes in returning the book to Cromwell, "that I have been so scrupulous, and as it were a picker of quarrels to his Grace's book, making a great matter of every light fault, or rather where no fault is at all; which I do only for this intent, that because the book now shall be set forth by his Grace's censure and judgment, I would have nothing therein that Momus could reprehend " (Jenkyns i. 227).

upon the Eucharist. They had mistaken their man. Cranmer's orthodoxy on the great subject, and Cranmer's sense of English independence, were alike affronted. He told the ambassadors that Atkinson should do his penance at St. Paul's and nowhere else. It was in vain that they pleaded that a condemned Saxon's life had been spared at the instance of Bishop Foxe, when he was in Germany. That error of the Sacrament of the Altar was so greatly spread in the realm, the Archbishop answered, and daily increasing more and more, that it was needful for the penance to be performed where the most people might be present, and thereby, in seeing him punished, to beware of the like offence. 1

It was not a hopeful episode at the beginning of an attempt at doctrinal agreement ; yet the sanguine Archbishop went forward. The committee appointed to confer with the Germans, of which he was one, discussed with them patiently HQ.Q greater part of the Augsburg Confession, and drafted a revised form of some of its Articles which seemed likely to be acceptable to both sides; but after that they diverged. 2 The German " orators " wished to proceed to the remaining Articles of Augsburg, which treated of the Mass, Communion in one kind, Confession, the priestly celibate, and the like, under the head of abuses. Cranmer was willing to be guided by their preference. But the other commissioners thought differently. The King himself, they said, was writing upon the alleged abuses, and they would not risk a difference from him. They demanded a discussion of Matrimony, Orders, Confirmation, and Extreme Unction, which found no place in the Augsburg Confession, and in which, as Cranmer affirms, " they 1 Jenkyns i. 249. 2 See Ibid, iv. 273.

know certainly that the Germans will not agree with us." Upon this shoal the negotiations were wrecked. Evidently the King was not pleased with the Germans, who seemed to suppose that they had come to teach, not to learn. If Cranmer was not misinformed, they were even treated with scanty courtesy. They were kept waiting month after month, in hopes of some final decision by the King. The princes who sent them began to chafe at the expense to which they were put. Lambeth was not in condition to receive them as guests, and the house assigned to them by Cromwell was far from agreeable. " Besides the multitude of rats," says Cranmer," daily and nightly running in their chambers, which is no small disquietness, the kitchen standeth directly against their parlour where they daily dine and sup; and by reason thereof the house savoureth so ill, that it offendeth all men that come into it." 1 The orators took their departure ; and though Burckhardt returned next year in a more open frame of mind, the scheme for corporate union never revived in the days of Henry. Archbishop Cranmer, whose wish was often father to his thought, had long persuaded himself that the King, as well as Cromwell, was altogether on his side in matters of religion. Soon after the departure of the Germ an "orators" in 1538, a lively correspondence broke forth between him and a Justice and Privy Councillor in his diocese, who claimed the " Bishops' Book " as an indication that Henry " allowed all the old fashions, and put all the knaves of the new learning to silence." Acting upon this opinion, the Councillor had endeavoured to stop the reading of the Bible, and at sessions molested the favourers of the Gospel. Cranmer 1 Jenkyns i. 264.

THE REFORMATION UNDER HENRY 109

warned him that if he did not change his ways, he should be constrained to complain of him to the King, " which (he says) I were very loth to do, and it is contrary to my mind and usage hitherto." Men like this Justice were so blinded, Cranmer said, that they called the old new, and the new old. " In very deed," he wrote, " the people be restored b$ this book to their good old usages, although they be nor, restored to their late abused usages. The old usage wa^s in the primitive Church, and nigh thereunto when the Church was most purest. If men will indifferently read these late declarations, they shall well perceive, that purgatory, pilgrimages, praying to saints, images, holy bread, holy water, holy days, merits, works, ceremonies, and such other, be not restored to their late accustomed abuses, but shall evidently perceive that the word of God hath gotten the upper hand of them all, and hath set them in their right use and estimation." If it were not for the favour that he bore him, the Archbishop said that he would call the Justice's servants before him as heretics, for all their brag. 1

He was soon to receive a painful surprise with regard to the King's attitude. Personally attached as the King was to Cranmer, he was by no means so much in love as Cranmer thought with reforming schemes. Ann Boleyn was gone. Cromwell, though still in favour, was no longer so necessary to the King. In June 1540, the "Whip with Six Strings" descended upon the shoulders of those who, in the main, looked to Cranmer as their leader.

It is strange that the Six Articles should have been considered to denote a great reactionary cha,nge in 1 Jenkyns i. 206 foil.

Henry's mind. 1 There is little in the doctrine which is not covered by the J Ten Articles, or the " Bishops' Book," or previous Mj unctions. They do indeed add Transubstantiation jjo the

.Real Presence, and affirm that communion in both kinds is unnecessary, and that private masses ought to be continued ; but these points were not denied in the earlier formularies. The need of auricular confession was more strongly inculcated in the " Bishops' Book " than in the Six Articles. In one respect only might men who watched Henry carefully feel a legitimate surprise at his new Act. When almost the last conventual establishments were closing, it was announced that vows of chastity, advisedly taken, were for ever binding. Otherwise, the Articles gave expression to Henry's consistent orthodoxy. But to those who interpreted Henry by what he had more or less tacitly allowed, the Articles were a terrible shock. These " Six new Articles of our Faith," says a contemporary, were " as well agreeing with the word of God and the former book of religion, called the 'Bishops' Book,' as fire with water, light with darkness, and Christ with Belial." [2]

Cranmer, at the beginning of the Parliament which passed these Articles, had been put on a small committee of divines who were to draw up a new declaration of Anglican belief. Before, however, they could arrive at any result, the Duke of Norfolk was sent by the King into the House of Lords with the draft of the Six Articles, and a bill to enforce them by fearful

[1] The anonymous " Life and Death of Cranmer " in Narratives of the Reformation (p. 224) ascribes the change to the desire of Cranmer and other bishops to rescue the monasteries from falling a prey to the King.

[a] Narratives of the Reformation p. 224.

THE REFORMATION UNDER HENRY III

penalties. Against this bill, Cranmer contended, according to his secretary's account, "most dangerously." [1] On three consecutive days, it is said, with the aid of the other reforming bishops, he maintained his ground. At last, Henry himself came down to the House to take the side against him. So powerful was Cranmer's opposition, that the King sent word to him to withdraw from the House of Lords, which the Archbishop respectfully declined to do. when the Act was passed, the King, who was capable of admiring a skilful argument, even when it was against himself, begged Cranmer to send him a copy of his speeches. By the Act itself, it had been made heresy, punishable at common law, to speak against the first of the Articles, and felony to speak against the rest. To commit his arguments to paper was therefore to run a good deal of risk; and an exciting adventure befell the book. Morice, the secretary, who wrote it out, was obliged one day to go over from Lambeth to London, and, for better safe-keeping, took the book with him. A bear-baiting was taking place at the time in a boat on the river. The bear broke loose, capsized Morice's wherry, plunged Morice into the Thames, and sent the book floating down the tide. It came into the hands of the bearward, who was a zealous Papist. When he found whose and what it was, the bearward thought he had found his opportunity against the heretical Archbishop. " You be like, I trust," he told the secretary, " to be both hanged for this book." Refusing to give it up for money, he carried it to the council-chamber, and only the fortunate interference of Cromwell prevented the man from bringing the matter to an issue. [2]

Henry's request for Cranmer's arguments had been conveyed by Cromwell and Norfolk, whom, after the passing of the Six Articles Bill, the King had sent to dine at Lambeth with the Archbishop, and to assure him that the King had not taken his outspokenness amiss. Henry knew well that Cranmer stood in need of consolation. He had not only suffered the defeat of principles which were dear to him. The Six Articles had touched him in a very tender spot. They had put an end to his married life. '

It ought, perhaps, to have been no great surprise to Cranmer that the law should be made more stringent against the marriage of the clergy. No permission of such marriage had at any time been given; and in 1538 a royak proclamation had been issued for depriving any priests/who were known to be married, and forbidding thera to " minister any sacrament or other ministry mysticay' 1 Notwithstanding this, an impression had been samehow created, that the King intended to allow priests to marry. 2 Perhaps Strype is right in thinking that the very wording of the prohibition— iages that be openly known" —was taken to mean! that marriages which were kept quiet would be unmolested. It came, therefore, as a thunderbolt to Crarimer and many others, when the third of the new Articles affirmed that God's law forbade the marriage of priests, whether before or after receiving that sacred order; and the Act declared such marriages void, and made them, if persisted in, a capital offence.

Cranmer's wife had, no doubt,been always kept in strict retirement. The scoffing Papists of Queen Mary's time

1 Wilkins iii. 696, where the date is wrongly given.

2 Strype's Cranmer i. 154.

THE REFORMATION UNDER HENRY 113

made merry over the shifts to which, in their imagination, the Archbishop had been put to hide her. All sorts of ludicrous situations were invented. He was said to have carried her about " in a great chest full of holes, that his pretty Nobsey might take breath at." x Now, however, even this precarious felicity could be eojoyed no more. Osiander's niece was shipped off to her friends in Germany, and the Archbishop had to work on as best he could without her. When his troubles with the Canons of Canterbury began, some three years after, the King, " putting on an air of pleasantry, asked him whether his bedchamber could stand the test of the Articles." Cranmer's straightforward answer pleased Henry. The King told him that the severity of the Act had not been levelled at him, and renewed his promises of favour. 2

On one point, indeed, the King had taken the Archbishop's part in the debate on the Six Articles. So clearly had Cranmer shown that auricular confession to a priest (which Cranmer valued and used) was not made compulsory on all men in Scripture, that when Bishop Tunstall sent in to the King afterwards a re-statement of his opinion to the contrary, Henry replied that he wondered at him. It had been proved, he said, both by the Bishop of Canterbury and himself, that the texts which Tunstall quoted " made smally or nothing to his purpose." 3

Within a year of the passing of the Six Articles Cromwell fell, accused of heresy, as well as of treason.

1 Harpsfield's Pretended Divorce of Henry VIII. p. 275. Cp. Bishop Crammer's Eecantacyons p. 8.

2 Collier v. 127.

3 Todd i. 276, from Bui-net.

At the moment when Cranmer wrote to the King in his defence, the Archbishop himself was in the thick of an unequal conflict on behalf of the very principles which helped to ruin the Vicegerent. A commission had again been appointed for formulating afresh the doctrine of the Church. "At that season," says his secretary, " the whole rabblement which he took to be his friends, being commissioners with him, forsook him and his opinion in doctrine, and so, leaving him post alone, revolted altogether." Gardiner was, of course, the leader of the opposition; but he was joined by Heath, who had won the testimonial of Melanchthon, by Day of Chichester, and others who owed their advancement to Cranmer. Heath, and Skip, Bishop of Hereford, as familiar friends of the Archbishop, took him down into the garden at Lambeth, and urged him to adopt a form of words which they thought more likely to find acceptance with the King than that which Cranmer pressed upon the committee. Cranmer bade them beware what they did. He told them that he knew the King's nature. The truth would one day come out about these articles; and then the King would never again trust those who had in false prudence concealed it from him. 1 Cranmer was right. While heavy odds were being laid by betting men in London that Cranmer, before Convocation broke up, would be set in the Tower beside his friend, Cromwell, " God gave him such favour with his Prince, that the book altogether passed, by his assertion, against all their minds." Henry's suspicions were aroused by the change of mind which he saw in others of the com-

1 Foxe viii. 24.

missioners; his regard for Cranmer's constancy " drave him all alone to join" with him. 1

This book, which the Archbishop carried through, was no other than the Necessary Doctrine and Erudition of a Christian Man, commonly called the " King's Book," to distinguish it from the " Bishops' Book." Most writers, considering the time at which it appeared to be a time of reaction, have been compelled to find in the " King's Book " a marked contrast to the doctrine of its predecessor. Morice's account of the circumstances of its birth puts a different construction upon the matter. So far from suggesting that the Necessary Erudition was the work of a retrograde party, authorised in spite of Cranmer's opposition, it shows that that book in the main represents the triumph of Cranmer, at a moment when he seemed most unlikely to succeed. 2

1 Morice Narratives of the Reformation p. 248.

2 The employment to which Foxe has put a part of Morice's graphic language has misled many subsequent writers. Foxe makes Cranmer to oppose the Six Articles "post alone." Morice, when he used that phrase, used it of Cranmer's position, not at the time of the Six Articles, but at the time of Cromwell's fall. Foxe uses it of an occasion when Cranmer was beaten; Morice of an occasion when Cranmer won. The Six Articles passed in 1539, a year before Cromwell fell. The only " book of articles of our religion " that we know of, which -was under discussion when Cromwell fell, was that which appeared in 1543 under the name of the Necessary Erudition. It is true that some slight detraction from Morice's authority at this point must be admitted, because of the evident signs that the old man's memory was here at fault in certain details. He mentions Thirlby (in the MS.) as one of those who deserted Cranmer, and then erases the name. He mentions Shaxton also, and leaves the name standing, although Shaxton had been forced to resign his see a year before. But Morice can hardly have been mistaken as to his main facts—that the book which then was carried was practically Cranmer's and that the other party were desirous of carrying something very different. No record remains of the alternative document which they favoured.

Nor, indeed, should any one be surprised that the Necessary Erudition, broadly speaking, represents Cranmer's views at the time of its composition. There are but few portions of it which are not taken from the earlier work, by a careful weaving together of material which in the earlier work was scattered and ill-arranged. There are, no doubt, passages in the new book which have the appearance of being due to Bishop Gardiner— as where the meaning of Latin words like Dominus, and fidelis, and ecclesia, and sanctorum, is discussed. Doubtless there are expressions which Cranmer must have deprecated, but the doctrine is not much changed. Transubstantiation is added to the Real Presence; but in mildly expressed terms, and Cranmer's objection to the doctrine had not yet formulated itself as it did a few years later. The Invocation of Saints is somewhat more encouraged than before; but it is carefully explained that their intercession is not efficacious except through the mediation of Christ, who is "the only eternal Priest and Bishop of His Church." In only one respect is Cranmer's private opinion markedly crossed. The new book maintains that priests ought not to marry; but Cranmer had already bowed to the Six Articles, when he found opposition unavailing. For the rest, the Necessary Erudition is avowedly a reforming work. It looks back with satisfaction upon what has been accomplished in that direction, although it admits that there has been evil mixed with the good. The condemnation of Rome is more emphatic than ever. The new sections on Faith, on Free WiVi, on Justification, on Good Works, are all written ^jfroin the standpoint of one who sympathises with th'£v lately recovered ideas upon those subjects, though soberly criticising the rash modes in

which they had been promulgated. On Penance, the book speaks in accordance with the views in which Cranmer and Henry were agreed. " The Sacrament of Penance " is boldly declared to be " properly the Absolution pronounced by the priest," to the obtaining of which contrition, confession, and satisfaction (usually considered to be the very elements of the sacrament) " be required as ways and means expedient and necessary." It would be very easy to imagine a presentment of Christian doctrine more reactionary than that which is commonly supposed to prove the revival of the party of the Old Learning. The "King's Book" may be taken to express fairly the English Reformation movement as guided by Cranmer under Henry VIII. 1

The mutual attachment between the two men lasted to the end. When Henry knew himself to be dying, he refused to see any divine except the Archbishop, for whom he sent in haste, but his power of speech was gone before the Archbishop arrived. " As soon as he came, the King stretched out his hand to him. The Archbishop exhorted him to place all his hope in the mercy of God through Christ, beseeching him earnestly that if he could not testify this hope in words, he would do so by a sign. Then the King wrung the

1 Although the Necessary Erudition must be considered to represent (with some deductions) the teaching of Cranmer, there is more reason for discerning a triumph of the Old Learning in the Rationale, an explanation of the Church services, which was drawn up at the same time. Who drew it up is quite uncertain; and I cannot think it likely to have been the work of the Commission on Ceremonies appointed by Cromwell in 1540 (see the list in Dixon ii/234). But it commended ceremonies which Cranmer did not love; and it may very probably be a proof of Cranmer's influence (as Strype affirms) that the Rationale was not adopted by the Church, as his Necessary Erudition was.

Archbishop's hand, which he held in his own, as hard as his failing strength would allow, and, directly after, breathed his last." l

The Archbishop's mourning for his master was deep and lasting, and he chose to wear the signs of it to his dying day. The fine portrait of him in the National Portrait Gallery, by an otherwise unknown painter-— Gerbic a Flicciis—was taken the year before Henry's death. It represents a large, clean-shaven man of fifty-seven years of age, sitting very upright in his chair. He does not look like a man of weak character, though the full and falling mouth might perhaps indicate some slowness of temperament. The brows are well-defined and slightly contracted, and the " purblind" eyes look inquiringly out from under them. In his hands are the Epistles of St. Paul, while on the table lies a book on Faith and Works. A later portrait would have represented him with a grey beard; for it is said that he never shaved his beard after the death of Henry, as a token of sorrow for his loss.

1 Godwin Eerum Angl. Annales p. 154 (ed. 1628).

CHAPTER IV

CRANMER UNDER EDWARD VI

THINGS changed rapidly after the death of Henry. Although the Archbishop had been put at the head of the Council of Regency by the will of the deceased King, the supreme power passed at once into the hands of the young Edward's uncle, best known as the Protector Somerset. It suited Somerset and his supporters to patronise the new ideas of religion, which promised to divert Church property to a most liberal extent for the use of lay lords. Before the year 1547 was out, a bill was passed in Parliament for granting to the King all chantries, colleges, and free chapels which had not already been dissolved. For some reason it was not till 1552 that the chantries were actually sold, by which time Somerset had fallen, and Northumberland had taken his place. Cranmer, who had formerly been distressed over the waste of the monastic property, strenuously opposed the meddling with the chantries. "He offered," says Morice, "to combat with the Duke of Northumberland, speaking on the behalf of his prince for the staying of the chantries until his Highness had come unto lawful age." 1 It was his own desire, as it must have been the desire of many, to maintain the

1 Narratives p. 247. 119

position of things which Henry had bequeathed, in other matters besides this of the chantries. Near the beginning of Edward's reign, he told Morice of the way in which Bishop Gardiner had hindered some reforms which he had nearly persuaded Henry to adopt; and when the secretary observed that he could now proceed with those reforms without obstruction, " Not so," the Archbishop replied; "it was better to attempt such reformation in King Henry VIII.'s days, than at this time, the King being in his infancy." *

But when it was determined by the dominant faction that the revolution was to go forward, Cranmer took up the cause and championed it. He did so not only because he was personally in favour of reform, but also in accordance with his consistent habit of deference to State authorities. Although the word is an unpleasant word to use of him, he was a thorough Erastian. It was a not uncommon nor strange position to adopt at that point in history. The English Church in past ' days had for a long while been accustomed to receive guidance and support from the Papacy; and when the Papacy could no longer be looked to, the royal power naturally took its place. Men like Tyndale, with whom Cranmer was in much sympathy, were ready to pay an extravagant deference to "the Prince." The Bible, which contained not a word about the Pope, had a great deal to say about the God-given authority of the King. To the King— especially the King of England—God had committed the responsibility of determining what was best for his subjects, in matters of religion, no less than in matters of ordinary policy. It was not that Cranmer held a low view of religion and 1 Foxe v. 563.

of its sanctions; it was that he held a high, an unwarrantably high, view of the State. The State, and the Head of the State, were to him so spiritual, so Divine, that ministers of religion, like himself, within the State, were bound, when it was not positively against their conscience, to submit their judgments to those who wielded the executive, and to carry out what was appointed them. The first thing which the Archbishop did on the accession of Edward was to take out a new license to exercise his archiepiscopal office; and so did Gardiner, Bonner, Tunstall, and the rest. He persisted in acting upon the same theory to the end, even when it cost him everything.

Bishop ^Gardiner was also an Erastian, but not so consistent an Erastian. Although, as Cranmer reminded him, he had once said that the King was as much King at one year old as at one hundred, as soon as he found that the platform of Henry VIII. was to be abandoned, he threw himself strenuously into opposition. When the Archbishop wrote to him to enlist his co-operation in bringing out the new Book of Homilies, which had been projected but not accomplished in Henry's reign, Gardiner utterly refused. The Necessary Erudition, he said, ought to be maintained as the standard of Christian teaching in the realm. To this Cranmer replied, in spite of the hand which he had had in the production of that book, that the King had been " seduced " into espousing it, and that Henry " knew by whom he was compassed." The many points in the book which represented Cranmer's triumph, shrank under Gardiner's provocation into insignificance beside the things in it which Cranmer disapproved. Gardiner retorted that after Cranmer had lived for four years in agreement

with the doctrine of the book, it was " a very strange speech " to say, so soon after King Henry's death, that his Highness was seduced. Not long after, the Bishop found himself in prison, and, though unjustly, laid his tribulations to the charge of Cranmer. The Archbishop was sincerely desirous to deliver him, and sent for him one day to the Deanery at St. Paul's. He spoke to him in defence of his Homily on Justification, to which Gardiner bad taken exception, hoping after all to persuade him to join in the projected Homilies. It was in vain. Gardiner confessed that he was no match for Cranmer in the argument. " He overcame me, that am called the Sophister," he said, "by sophistry;" but he would not co-operate, for all that. Cranmer was vexed with him. " You like nothing," he said, "unless you do it yourself." Nevertheless he endeavoured to overcome by kind offers what he thought to be personal obstinacy. " You are," he said, " a man meet in my opinion to be called to the Council again: we daily choose and add others that were not appointed by our late Sovereign Lord." " These," wrote Gardiner to Somerset, " were worldly comfortable words," but he thanked God there was not that deceit in him, which Cranmer seemed to think. 1 Such disputes threw the Archbishop all the more into the arms of the men who reigned in the King's name.

Upon another doctrine of great importance Cran-mer's opinion was now fast diverging from that of Gardiner. It was the doctrine of the Holy Eucharist. No doubt there were abuses in connexion with that sacrament which a.t any time of his life he would have wished to see rectified; and in all probability for 1 Dixon ii. 448, from Foxe.

a longer period than he himself was aware, he had been insensibly modifying his own conceptions of the mystery. But he had been content to use the current phraseology—and more than that, he believed himself to be wholly on the side of the teaching which then held the field. Soon after his accession to Canterbury, Frith had been brought before him (and others) to answer for his doctrine on Purgatory and on the Eucharist. Frith, though he had his own opinion about the Eucharistic Presence, yet did not maintain that it was the only lawful opinion; he did but maintain that neither was Transubstantiation the only lawful opinion. " This article " he wrote from prison, " is 110 necessary article of faith. I grant that neither part is an article necessary to be believed under pain of damnation, but leave it as a thing indifferent, to think thereon as God shall instil in every man's mind, and that neither part condemn other for this matter, but receive each other in brotherly love, reserving each other's infirmity to God." l It would have been well if, in the controversy of which this was the first act, the spirit of these noble words could have been preserved. But Cranmer thought Frith entirely in the wrong; and although he was no more to blame for his execution than others were, he seems to have concurred fully in the judgment. " Other news have we none notable," he wrote to a friend abroad, "but that one Frith, which was in the Tower in prison, was appointed by the King's Grace to be examined before me" and others; " whose opinion was so notably erroneous that we could not despatch him, but was fain to leave him to the determination of his ordinary, which is the Bishop of 1 Dixon i. 168.

London. His said opinion is of such nature that he thought it not necessary to be believed as an article of our faith "—Cranmer notes accurately the position held by Frith—" that there is the very corporal presence of Christ within the host and sacrament of the altar, and holdeth of this point most after the opinion of Oeco-lampadius. And surely I myself sent for him three or four times to persuade him to leave that his imagination ; but for all that we could do therein, he would not apply to any counsel. Notwithstanding, now he is at a final end with examinations; for my Lord of London hath given sentence, and delivered him to the secular power, where he iooketh every day to go unto the fire." 1 So little sympathy had the Archbishop at that date with Oecolampadian views.

It was about four years later, that he wrote a Latin letter to Vadianus, a Swiss opponent of the real Presence, in terms of admiration and brotherliness indeed, but very earnest and decided upon the main contention.

" Frankly to tell you my mind (as good men ought to do with one another), the thesis which you maintain in those six books, of which you made me a present, is one which I do not like at all, and I wish you had spent your midnight labour to better purpose. Unless plainer proof can be given me than I have yet seen, I will be neither a patron nor an abettor of your opinions. I have seen everything, or nearly so, that Oecolampadius or Zwinglius have written and published, and I have learned that everything, no matter by what author, must be read with a critical eye. As far as they have endeavoured to point out, and refute, and amend, papistical and sophistical errors and abuses, I admire 1 Jenk\'7d 7 ns i. 31.

and approve. I wish they had stopped at those limits, and had not trampled down the wheat along with the tares. I do not think any fair reader will be convinced that the ancient authors are on your side in this controversy. If this is an error, it is one commended to us by the Fathers and by the Apostolic men themselves; and what good man could listen to such a statement, not to speak of believing it ? No words can express how this bloody controversy has everywhere, but among us particularly, hindered the Gospel word which was running so well. With your leave I exhort and advise you, nay, I pray and beseech, and in the bowels of Jesus Christ obtest and adjure you, to allow to the Churches that peace of God which passeth all understanding, that with united forces we may propagate the one sound, pure, evangelical doctrine, which is in accordance with the discipline of the primitive Church. We shall with ease convert even the Turks to the obedience of our Gospel, if we can but agree among ourselves." 1

It was believed by some in Cranmer's own time, and has been asserted again in ours, that the Archbishop passed from the belief in Transubstantiation to his later doctrine, through a phase of Lutheran opinion on the subject. " You, Mr. Cranmer," said Martin to him at his trial, " have taught in this high sacrament of the altar three contrary doctrines." " Nay," he answered ; " I taught but two contrary doctrines in the same." 2 From his own point of view he was speaking the exact truth. There was no period at which he taught a definite doctrine like Luther's, opposed to the Roman on the one hand, and to the Swiss one on the other. The Lutheran dogma of Consubstantiation is a highly elaborated dogma, 1 Jenkyns i. 193. 2 Ibid. iv. 95.

of which it is hardly unfair to say that it unites the difficulties of both the other theories of Cranmer's time without the advantages of either. So little sympathy with it was felt in England, that Ridley affirmed that the Papists and he were more nearly agreed together than either of them was with the Lutherans; for while both he and the Papists affirmed that there was only one substance in the sacrament, the Lutherans affirmed that there were two. This theory Cranmer never held. Although in the first year of Edward VI.'s reign he published a translation of a Catechism on the subject by an avowed Lutheran, yet that Catechism does not give expression to the Lutheran dogma of Consubstan-tiation.

Yet there are not wanting indications that there was a time when Archbishop Cranmer was shaken in the doctrine of Transubstantiation, while abhorring the position he afterwards came to occupy. The year after his letter to Vadianus — in which year also Lambert was burned for holding Zwinglian opinions,—a preacher named Damplip came into trouble at Calais (which was in Canterbury diocese) for his Eucharistic teaching. The Archbishop wrote to Cromwell in his defence. " He utterly denieth that he ever taught or said that the very body and blood of Christ was not presently in the sacrament of the altar, and confesseth the same to be there really; but he saith that the controversy between him and the Prior was, because he confuted the opinion of the Transubstantiation; and therein I think he taught but the truth." 1 Cranmer had evidently begun to feel that it was possible to believe in the real Presence without holding Transubstan-1 Jenkyns, i. 257 (August 15, 1538).

tiation — or Consubstantiation either. It was the opinion of others besides himself. Bishop Tunstall held the same view. He told his nephew, Bernard Gilpin, that Innocent III. had been "greatly overseen " in pressing Transubstantiation upon the Church. 1 Redmayne, the first Master of Trinity, who certainly never rejected the real Presence, said on his deathbed (1551), that he had studied the matter for twelve years, and found that some of the Fathers had written plainly contrary to Transubstantiation, and that in others it was not taught nor maintained. 2 " I confess of myself," wrote Cranmer at a later time, " that not long before I wrote the said Catechism, I was in that error of the real Presence, as I was many years past in divers other errors, as of Transubstantiation "—which shows that he clearly distinguished between the two things—" for the which and other mine offences in youth I do daily pray unto God for mercy and pardon, saying, Delicta iuventutis meae et ignorantias meas ne memineris, Domine." 3

From that lofty ground where he was disposed to take his stand, believing on the one hand the real Presence in the sacrament, and on the other hand rejecting the mediaeval fiction of Transubstantiation, Archbishop Cranmer was dragged down by Nicholas Ridley. " I grant," he said at the end of his life, " that then (when he wrote his catechism) I believed otherwise than I do now: and so I did until my Lord of London did confer with me, and by sundry persuasions and authorities of doctors, drew me quite from my opinion." 4 The new opinion which he embraced was embodied in a book published in the year 1550, and

1 Gilpin's Gilpin 170. 2 See Foxe vi. 267 foil.
3 Jenkyns iii. 13. 4 Ibid. iv. 97.

entitled, " A Defence of the true and Catholic Doctrine of the Sacrament of the Body and Blood of our Saviour Christ, with a confutation of sundry errors concerning the same, grounded and established upon God's Holy Word, and approved by the consent of the most ancient Doctors of the Church." It was not difficult for a man of Cranmer's reading and acumen to expose the absurdities of Transubstantiation, and of the Propitiatory Sacrifice, as then popularly understood. No one has done it more trenchantly. This part of his work is full of powerful sentences which deserve to be remembered:—

" Although all the accidents, both of the bread and wine, remain still, yet (say they) the same accidents be in no manner of thing. For in the body and blood of Christ (say they) these accidents cannot be; for the body and blood of Christ be neither of that bigness, fashion, smell, nor colour, that the bread and wine be. Nor in the bread and wine (say they) these accidents cannot be; for the substance of bread and wine (as they affirm) be clean gone. And so there remaineth whiteness, but nothing is white; there remaineth roundness, but nothing is round; and there is bigness, and yet nothing is big; there is sweetness, without any sweet thing; softness, without any soft thing; breaking, without anything broken; and so other qualities and quantities, without anything to receive them. And this doctrine they teach as a necessary article of our faith." 1 "If Christ would have had us believe, as a necessary article of our faith, that there remaineth neither bread nor wine, would He have spoken after this sort, using all such terms and circumstances as should 1 Jenkyns ii. 309.

make us believe that still there remaineth bread and wine ? " 1 " Our faith teacheth us to believe things that we see not; but it doth not bid us that we shall not believe that we see daily with our eyes." 2 "Let all these papists together show any one authority, either of Scripture or of ancient author, Greek or Latin, that saith as they say, that Christ called not bread and wine His body and blood, but indimduum vagum (a particular thing uncertain), and for my part I shall give them place, and confess that they say true/' 3 In the " doctrine of the old Catholic Church " is " no absurdity nor inconvenience, nothing spoken either contrary to Holy Scripture or to natural reason, philosophy, or experience, or against any old ancient author." 4 " No man (says Theodoret) ought to be so arrogant and presumptuous to affirm for a certain truth in religion anything which is not spoken of in Holy Scripture. And this is spoken to the great and utter condemnation of the papists, which make and unmake new articles of our faith from time to time, at their pleasure, without any Scripture at all. And yet will they have all men bound to believe whatsoever they invent, upon peril of damnation and everlasting fire." 5

Cranmer was not, however, so successful in his constructive attempts, as in his criticism of the views of others. The doctrine which he now inculcated was practically indistinguishable from that of Oecolampadius It is true that he will not allow it to be said that he makes the sacramental emblems mere emblems. " The sacramental bread and wine be not bare and naked

1 Jenkyns ii. 316. 2 Ibid. 318.
3 Ibid. 376. 4 Ibid. 358.
5 Ibid. 395.

figures, but so pithy and effectuous, that whosoever worthily eateth them eateth spiritually Christ's flesh and blood, and hath by them everlasting life." l But, nevertheless, the body of Christ is " absent." Cranmer does not hesitate to use the word. "The eating and drinking of Christ's flesh and blood is not taken in the common signification, with mouth and teeth to eat and chew a thing being present, but by a lively faith, in heart and mind, to chew and digest a thing being absent." 2 "It is a figurative speech, spiritually to be understand, that we must deeply print and fruitfully believe in our hearts that His flesh was crucified and His blood shed for our redemption. And this our belief in Him is to eat His flesh and to drink His blood, although they be not present here with us but be ascended into heaven." 3 The only sense in which Cranmer will allow that Christ's body is present with us at the Eucharist, is that in which the sun is present upon the earth, by its light and heat. 4 It is only a virtual presence, and that, not in the sacrament, but in the worthy receivers of the sacrament. Christ is no otherwise present with us in the Eucharist than He is in Baptism; 5 and the bread is only called His body in the same way that any other figure bears the name of the things it figures:—" as a man's image is called a man," he writes, " a lion's image a lion, and an image of a tree and herb is called a tree or herb. So were we wont to say, Our Lady of Walsingham; Great St. Christopher of York or Lincoln; Our Lady smileth or rocketh her Child; and a thousand like speeches, which were not understood of the very things, but only of the images of them." 6

1 Jenkyns ii. 422. 2 Ibid. 378. 3 Ibid. 381.
4 Ibid. 358. & Ibidm 413> 416< 6 MM 44(X

It would be unfair not to add that in spite of this low conception of the Eucharistic Presence, there are many beautiful passages in the book, showing that Cranmer's actual devotion to the Holy Sacrament was not impaired. The language of Ignatius and Irenaeus, which his opponents thought to be on their side, was not too glowing for Cranmer. " Neither they," he says, " nor no man else, can extol and commend the same sufficiently, if it be godly used as it ought to be." 1 Again and again he speaks of its daily use as if it were the obvious and natural thing. Christ ordained, he says, "not a yearly memory (as the Paschal lamb was eaten but once a year), but a daily remembrance He ordained in bread and wine sanctified and dedicated to that purpose." 2 Christ's sacrifice "is figured, signified, and represented unto us by that bread and wine which faithful people receive daily in the Holy Communion." 3 The reception of Christ, though purely spiritual, was not the less real or less awful. "Although He sit in heaven, at His Father's right hand, yet should we come to this mystical bread and wine with faith, reverence, purity, arid fear, as we would do if we should come to see and receive Christ Himself sensibly present. For unto the faithful, Christ is at His own holy table present with His mighty Spirit and grace, and is of them more fruitfully received, than if corporally they should receive Him bodily present. And, therefore, they that shall worthily come to this God's board, must after due trial of themselves consider, first, who ordained this table, also what meat and drink they shall have that come thereto, and how they ought to behave themselves

thereat. He that prepared the table is Christ Himself. The meat and drink wherewith He feedeth them that come thereto as they ought to do, is His own flesh and blood. They that come thereto must occupy their minds in considering how His body was broken for them, and His blood shed for their redemption. And so ought they to approach to this heavenly table with all humbleness of heart and godliness of mind, as to the table wherein Christ Himself is given." 1

It is a genuine spiritual prompting which impels the author, who is jealous "lest that in the stead of Christ Himself be worshipped the sacrament." 2 The customary worship was, in his belief, a " horrible idolatry, to worship things visible and made with their own hands," when people adored what were, on their own theory, only accidents and not the very substance itself. " Else," he says, " what made the people to run from their seats to the altar, and from sacring (as they called it) to sacring, peeping, tooting, and gazing at that thing which the priest held up in his hands, if they thought not to honour that thing which they saw ? What moved the priests to lift up the sacrament so high over their heads ? or the people to cry to the priest, * Hold up, hold up'! and one man to say to another, ' Stoop down before '; or to say, ' This day have I seen my Maker'; and,' I cannot be quiet except I see my Maker once a day' ? If they worshipped nothing that they saw, why did they rise up to see ?" 3 The error of Rome, he said, lay in " not bringing them by bread unto Christ, but from Christ unto bread." 4

It was no innate love of controversy which induced

1 Jenkyns ii. 438. 2 Ibid. 441.
3 Ibid. 442. 4 Ibid. 446.

Cranmer to take up his pen in this matter, but the solemn sense of his high and providential office. " God I take to witness," he writes, " who seeth the hearts of all men throughly to the bottom, that I take this labour for none other consideration, but for the glory of His name, and the discharge of my duty, and the zeal that I bear toward the flock of Christ. I know in what office God hath placed me, and to what purpose; that is to say, to set forth His word truly unto His people, to the uttermost of my power. I know what account I shall make to Him hereof at the last day, when every man shall answer for his vocation, and receive for the same good or ill, according as he hath done. It pitieth me to see the simple and hungry flock of Christ led into corrupt pastures, to be carried blindfold they know not whither, and to be fed with poison in the stead of wholesome meats." 1

This work of Archbishop Cranmer's was originally called forth by a treatise of Bishop Gardiner's, entitled A Detection of the Devil's Sophistry ; and it called forth in turn a reply from Gardiner, to which Cranmer answered once more, sentence by sentence, from beginning to end.

Gardiner was not a profound or well-read divine; and he approached the subject from the point of view of a man of common sense, who accepts the traditional opinion in a broad way, without caring to go into the niceties of it. The consequence is that the Archbishop has no difficulty in showing that there are grave and frequent differences between the Bishop and the authorities whom he supposed himself to follow.

"There was never man of learning that I have read," says the common-sense Gardiner, "termed the matter 1 Jenkyns ii. 289.

so, that Christ goeth into the stomach of the man that receiveth, and no further." "It is marvel," replies the Archbishop, "that you never read [this], being a lawyer, and seeing that it is written in the Gloss of the law De Consecr. dist. ii. Tribus Gradibus in these words—' It is certain that as soon as the forms be torn with the teeth, so soon the body of Christ is gone up into heaven And if you had read Thomas de Aquino and Bonaventure (great clerks and holy saints of the Pope's own making) with other school authors, then should you have known what the papists do say in this matter. For some say that the body of Christ remaineth, although it be in a dog, or mouse. And some say it is not in the mouse or dog, but remaineth only in the person that eateth it, until it be digested in the stomach. Some say it remaineth no longer than the sacrament is in the eating, and may be felt, seen, and tasted in the mouth. And this, besides Hugo, saith Pope Innocentius himself, who was the best learned and chief doer in this matter of all the other popes. Read you never none of these authors, and yet take upon you the full knowledge of this matter? Will you take upon you to defend the papists and know not what they say?"[1] "This is marvellous rhetoric," says the layman-like Bishop, when Cranmer has affirmed that the papists say "that in the sacrament the corporal members of Christ be not distant in place from one another, but wheresoever the head is, there be the feet." "This is marvellous rhetoric, and such as the author hath overseen himself[2] in the utterance of it, and eon-fesseth himself prettily abused, to the latter end of his years to have believed that [which] he now calleth so 1 Jenkyns iii. 101. 2 Made a mistake.

foolish. This author impudently beareth in hand l the Catholic Church to teach that [which] he listeth to bear in hand may by wanton reason be deduced of their teaching; whereas all true Christian men believe simply Christ's words, and trouble not their heads with such consequences as seem to strive with reason." "This is such matter as were not tolerable to be by a scoffer devised in a play, to supply when his fellow had forgotten his part." "I bear not the Church in hand, as you report of me/' replies the Archbishop, "that it saith and teacheth that whole Christ is in every part of the bread consecrated, bat I say that the papists so teach. And because you deny it, read the chief pillars of all the papists, Duns and Thomas de Aquino, who say that Christ is whole under every part of the forms of bread and wine, not only when the host is broken, but when it is whole also. And there is no distance, saith he, of parts one from another, as of one eye from another, or the eye from the ear, or the head from the feet. These be Thomas's words. And not only the papists do thus write and teach, but the Pope himself, Innocentius III. And yet you say, the Church saith not so; which I affirm also; and then it must needs follow that the doctrine of the papists is not the doctrine of the Church." "And so the whole doctrine of the papists, which they have taught these four or five hundred years, do you condemn with condign reproaches, as a teaching intolerable, not to be devised by a scoffer in a play."[2] "This author," says the indignant Gardiner, "findeth fault that the priest's devotion should be a sacrifice satisfactory, and not the

1 Tries to make us believe.
2 Pp. 113, 118 foil., 145 foil.

thing that is offered, which manner of doctrine I never read, and I think it myself it ought to be improved, 1 if any such there he to make the devotion of the priest a satisfaction. For undoubtedly Christ is our satisfaction wholly and fully." "Although you never read," returns his merciless censor, " that the oblation of the priest is satisfactory by devotion of the priest, yet nevertheless the papists do so teach, and you may find it in their St. Thomas, both in his Sum and upon the fourth of the Sentences, whose works have been read in the universities almost this three hundred years, and never until this day reproved by any of the papists in this point. He saith—' The sacrifice of the priest hath a satisfactory power; but in the satisfaction the mind of the offerer is more regarded than the greatness of the thing which he offereth.' " 2 The inexorable Primate gathers up a list of twenty articles in which Gardiner's ignorant good sense betrayed him into differing from accredited teachers on the same side.

 As a piece of dialectic against Gardiner, and against the mediaeval notions of the Eucharist generally, Cranmer's work is triumphant in almost every detail; and in order rightly to judge of his doctrine on the subject it is necessary to realise how degraded and material was the general opinion of the Mass at the time. It is not hard to understand how, when once a mind like his had persuaded itself to allow that the usual definitions of the Eucharistic Presence were wrong, no intermediate position would for long seem satisfactory. Craiimer swung to the opposite extreme. He would not in honesty give less than their fullest force to those expressions in Scripture and in the 1 Reprobated, 2 Pp. 150, 156.

 Fathers which seemed to treat the mystery as nothing but a virtual presence and a commemorative token. It was an interpretation as one-sided as that which Cranmer had discarded. But his readjustment of belief never made him irreverent towards the sacred ordinance, nor was he conscious of any departure from loyalty to the teaching of the primitive Church.

 The evolution of Cranmer's opinion on this subject was narrowly watched and criticised by many other observers besides Gardiner and his party. Every sign that he gave was chronicled for the information of foreign divines, especially of Bullinger, who had succeeded Zwingli at Zurich. The friends of the Swiss dictator were at first much dissatisfied with Cranmer, and lost no opportunity of telling Bullinger how little opinion the Archbishop had of him. "As to Canterbury," writes Traheron in August 1548, " he conducts himself in such a way that the people do not think much of him, and the nobility regard him as lukewarm. In other respects he is a kind, good-natured man/' 1 " This Thomas," wrote John ab Ulmis in the same month, " has fallen into so heavy a slumber, that we entertain but a very cold hope that he will be aroused even by your learned letter. He has lately published a Catechism, in which he has not only approved that foul and sacrilegious Transubstantiation of the Papists, but all the dreams of Luther seem to him well grounded, perspicuous, and lucid." 2 In September, they thought things looked more promising. " Latimer," wrote Traheron, " has come over to our opinion respecting the true doctrine of the Eucharist, together with the Archbishop of Canterbury and the other Bishops who here-1 Oriy. Letters p. 320. 2 Ibid. p. 381.

 tofore seemed to be Lutherans." l In December, Traheron was elated by Cranmer's language in the debate about the new Prayerbook. " The Archbishop of Canterbury," he wrote to Bullinger, " contrary to general expectation, most openly, firmly, and learnedly maintained your opinion upon this subject. I perceive that it is all over with Lutheranism." 2 But alas, the sanguine writer was obliged to add a postscript to his letter: " The foolish bishops have made a marvellous recantation." Peter Martyr, who was at that time regarded as a Lutheran, and who was present at the debate, felt no reason to be alarmed. " The palm," he wrote to Bucer, "remains with our friends, especially with the Archbishop of Canterbury, whom they till now were wont to traduce as a man ignorant of theology, and only conversant with matters of government. But now, believe me, he has shown himself a mighty theologian. Transubstantiation, I think, is now exploded/ 5 3 It seemed as if Lutheranism was about to triumph when Bucer himself came to this country. " Bucer and Paul Fagius," writes Burcher to Bullinger in the following May, " have safely arrived in England, and have written from the palace of the Archbishop of Canterbury. I wish they may not pervert him, or make him worse." 4 " When I gave your letter to the Archbishop of Canterbury," writes Hooper, also in May, " he did not vouchsafe a single word respecting either yourself, or your godly Church. Bucer has very great influence with him, and the Archbishop will appoint him to the Regius Professorship at Cambridge." 5 But by the end of the year, Switzerland had beaten Ger-

1 Orig. Letters p. 322. B Ibid. p. 323.
8 Ibid. p. 470. 4 Ibid. p. 652. 5 Ibid. p. 64.

many, though there was still room for anxiety. " The Archbishop of Canterbury," wrote Hooper, " entertains right views as to the nature of Christ's presence in the Supper, and is now very friendly towards myself. He has some articles of religion, to which all preachers are required to subscribe; and in these his sentiments respecting the Eucharist are pure and religious, and similar to yours in Switzerland. We desire nothing more for him than a firm and manly spirit. Like all the other Bishops in this country, he is too fearful about what may happen to him." 1 By 1551, Hooper (himself then a bishop) could tell Bullinger that Cranmer was hardly able to refrain from tears at receiving a letter from him. " He made most honourable mention both of yourself and of your profound erudition. You have no one, I am sure, among all your dearest friends, who is more interested about you, and loves you in Christ more ardently." 2

The history of Archbishop Cranmer's opinion with regard to the Holy Eucharist is of importance not only because of its bearing upon his last end, but because of his permanent influence upon the Church of England by means of the Book of Common Prayer. Perhaps no part of his work had such an interest for the Archbishop as the liturgical reform, and certainly there was none for which posterity has more reason to be grateful to him. The history of the Prayerbook down to the end of Edward's reign is the biography of Cranmer, for there can be no doubt that almost every line of it is his composition.

It was a task for which he was well fitted. So far as the study was possible in that age, Cranmer was a student l Orig. betters p. 72. 2 Ibid. p. 93,

of comparative liturgiology. " A singularly clear answer to the supposition not unfrequently entertained, that he was not well informed about liturgical order and ritual propriety, may be given," says Mr. Burbidge, " by putting into the hands of his critics his copy of Gemma Animae, or Dircctorium Sacerdotum secundwm usum Sarum, or Erasmus's version of the Liturgy of St. Chrysostom; and by offering them a choice of his editions of Durandus's Rationale Divinorum Officiorum." l It was Cranmer who introduced into the West the now familiar " Prayer of St. Chrysostom." Some features of the Second Prayerbook were very probably due to his acquaintance with the Mozarabic offices of Spain. 2 He had paid attention to the various old English uses, some of which would have been lost to memory if he had not happened to mention them in his Preface to the Prayerbook. That Preface was largely taken—as well as many hints for the daily offices—from the reforming Breviary of Cardinal Quignon. The attempts of Hermann, Archbishop of Cologne, were followed with deep interest by his brother Archbishop, and the result is very apparent in our Occasional Offices. And if Cranmer was qualified for liturgical revision by special studies, he was no less qualified by his splendid command of the English language, and by his instinctive sense of what would suit average English minds. His genius for devotional composition in English is universally recognised, even by those who have least sympathy with his character and career.

As early as 1543—the year of the Necessary Erudition —he had announced King Henry's intention of taking

1 Liturgies and Offices of the Church p. xiv.
2 See Burbidge Liturgies and Offices pp. 175, 196.

some steps in the reform of the service books, and it was prescribed that a Lesson should be read in English morning and evening, after Te Deum and Magnificat\'7d-The year after, Cranmer was employed in composing English Litanies, or " Processions," and a deeply interesting letter of his is preserved, in which he says to the King—

" According to your Highness's commandment, I have translated into the English tongue, so well as I could in so short time, certain processions, to be used upon festival days, if after due correction and amendment of the same your Highness shall think so convenient. In which translation, forasmuch as many of the processions in the Latin were but barren, as me seemed, and little fruitful, I was constrained to use more than the liberty of a translator. Some processions I have added whole, because I thought I had better matter for the purpose than was the procession in Latin; the judgment whereof I refer wholly to your Majesty. And after your Highness hath corrected it, if your Grace command some devout and solemn note to be made thereunto, I trust it will much excitate and stir the hearts of all men unto devotion and godliness." After some recommendations about the music, he adds— " As concerning the Salve festa dies, the Latin note, as I think, is sober and distinct enough; wherefore I have travailed to make the verses in English, and have put the Latin note unto the same. Nevertheless, they that be cunning in singing can make a much more solemn note thereto. I made them only for a proof, to see how English would do in song. But because mine English verses lack the grace and facility that I would wish they 1 Wilkins iii. 863.

had, your Majesty may cause some other to make them again, that can do the same in more pleasant English and phrase." 1

Except for the publication of an authorised Primer (or book of Private Devotions) in 1546, which was intended to supersede all other Primers, no more was done in the direction of reforming the services during Henry VIII.'s reign. Projects there were, however, for further action, Cranmer told Morice, and Morice told Foxe, of a conversation which took place at Hampton Court in August 1546, when "the great ambassador" came from Francis I. to Henry. " After the banquet was done the first night, the King was leaning upon the ambassador and upon me. If I should tell what communication was had, concerning the establishment of sincere religion then, a man would hardly have believed it; nor had I myself thought the King's Highness had been so forward in these matters as then appeared. I may tell you it passed the pulling down of roods, and suppressing the ringing of bells. I take it that few in England would have believed that the King's Majesty and the French King had been at this point, within half a year after to have changed the Mass in both the realms into a Communion, as we now use it. And herein the King's Highness willed me (quoth the Archbishop) to pen a form thereof to be sent to the French King to consider of." 2 But the deaths

1 On the question of the date of this letter, see Jenkyns i. 316. The translation of Salve festa dies is unhappily lost. It is not improbable that we have a specimen of Cranmer's translation into metre in the longer version of Veni Creator Spiritus in the Ordinal," though it has undergone modification (see Julian's Dictionary of Hymnoloqy 1209).

2 Foxe v. 563.

first of Henry and then of Francis broke off the scheme.

Notwithstanding the reluctance, which Cranmer at first showed, to make or allow innovations during Edward's minority, he was soon found endeavouring to execute what had thus been suggested by Henry. Before the end of the year in which Henry died, it was unanimously determined by Convocation that the Communion should be administered to all Christians under both kinds; and by March of the following year (1548), the new Order of the Communion appeared, which, while it retained the old Latin service of the Mass, surrounded it with English exhortations and devotions, most of which still stand in our Prayerbook. They are mainly based upon the " Consultation " of Archbishop Hermann of Cologne, which had been translated into English and was familiarly known to the Archbishop. Before the last month of 1548 ran out, Parliament had approved the First Prayerbook of Edward VI., which received the encomiums of Bishop Gardiner, and which probably constituted the " marvellous recantation" of Swiss principles complained of by Traheron to Bullinger.

But scarcely was the First Prayerbook published, when its chief author began to prepare for a second. He was already surrounded by foreign divines—some of whom had taken refuge in England from troubles abroad, some came on Cranmer's invitation. A Lasco, Bucer, Peter Martyr, Fagius, Ochino, Tremellius, were among the more distinguished of the company. To the list of foreigners who surrounded Cranmer must be added the name of the Scotch Calvinist, John Knox. " We desire," wrote the Archbishop to Hardenberg in

July 1548, "to set before our Churches the true theology, and we have decided that we need the presence of learned men, to compare their decisions with ours, so as to do away with doctrinal controversies, and build up a whole body of true doctrine. We have summoned a great many godly and learned men, some of whom we have already got, and expect others soon." 1 To induce Melanchthon to come was an object of repeated and earnest effort. " If," says Cranmer, " when a similar appeal was made to him by that holy old Elector of Cologne, he resolved not to turn a deaf ear to it, surely he will feel bound to listen now, in a case of far greater importance and urgency." He desired to hold a Pan-evangelical Council, in opposition to that which was assembled at Trent. " Our adversaries," he wrote to Calvin, "are now holding their Council at Trent for the establishing of errors, and shall we fail to assemble a godly synod to refute errors, and to purify and propagate our doctrines ? They, I hear, are making decrees regarding Bread-worship; therefore we ought to leave no stone unturned, not only to protect others against this idolatry, but also to come to an agreement among ourselves upon the doctrine of this sacrament. With your powers of observation you cannot but see how much the Church of God is weakened by dissensions and differences of opinion regarding this sacrament of unity. I am anxious for agreement in this doctrine, not only about the subject itself, but also about the very words and forms of expression." 2 Not only Calvin and Melanchthon, but Bullinger also, received letters from Canterbury to aid in the great project.

Those three illustrious personages could not, or did 1 Jenkyns i. 332. 2 Ibid. 346.

not, come; but two of them wrote their minds, and altogether Cranmer had no lack of foreign advice. In 1552 (an English Ordinal having in the meantime been completed and put in use) the Second Prayerbook, which was in all its main points our present book, was ordered to be used, after receiving the criticisms of Bucer and others. It shows how far the Archbishop was prepared to go in satisfying the extreme innovators. As regards the main question of the day, the Eucharistic service was entirely rearranged. While the First Prayerbook had followed in the main the order of the pre-reformation service, the new one was upon an altogether original plan. All direct invocation of the Holy Spirit upon the sacramental elements was omitted. The great intercession was no longer connected with the Consecration. The Lord's Prayer, with its significant petition for the Christian's Daily Bread, was placed after the Communion, and no longer before it. So was the G-loria in JExcelsis. There was no longer any explicit prayer for the faithful departed. The sacrificial character of the Eucharist does not depend upon any special prayers or ceremonies that may be performed or uttered in the course of the service, but resides in the celebration of the sacrament as a whole, and no action of the liturgical reformers could get rid of it; but this aspect of the service was as much obscured as could easily be done.

And yet the Second Prayerbook itself is a monument of the moderation of Archbishop Cranmer. If there are in it omissions which Catholic-minded men may regret, yet there is not a single phrase in it which a Catholic-minded man need hesitate to use. The service is rich and ample in comparison with

L

anything which foreign reformed communities use. Although Cranmer himself once or twice speaks somewhat slightingly of "consecration," yet in the liturgy he made the recital of the words of institution to form part of a Prayer of Consecration, instead of the bare reading of them to the congregation, which was all that the foreign bodies permitted. While Luther-anism forbade the celebrant of the Eucharist to receive the sacrament himself, because that was looked upon as the consummation of the sacrifice, the English book laid it down—"Then shall the minister first receive the Communion in both kinds himself." Although the words used at the delivery of the sacrament were not what the Church had hitherto used, yet the scriptural " Take and eat this," " Drink this," were not narrowed by any interpretative addition, such as "this bread," " this wine." The more impressive and special vestments prescribed in the first book were laid aside in the second; yet the bishop's rochet and the presbyter's surplice remained, to the scandal of most of the Swiss party. Provision continued to be made that the " solemn note " which Cranmer loved should be used to " excitate devotion." And in spite of all his invective against "artolatry," the Archbishop inserted in the Second Prayerbook (what had not been thought necessary to mention in the First) a rubric to say that the communicants were to be " kneeling" at the moment of reception. He knew what he was about in inserting that rubric. Hooper, A Lasco, and others, had already been denouncing the posture. John Knox alarmed the Council by the vehemence with which he took the same side. The all-powerful Council stopped the issue of the Prayerbook, and bade Cranmer call to him Ridley

and Peter Martyr, or such-like, and " weigh the prescription of kneeling." Cranmer replied that he would consult with them, but that he trusted " that we with just balance weighed this at the making of the book," and added that the Council were not wise to wish to alter the book at the motion of " these glorious and unquiet spirits," who would still find faults if the book were "made every year anew." In spite of storms of opposition, he would not hear of allowing communicants to stand or sit; he said they might as well " lie down on the ground and eat their meat like Turks or Tartars." The " Black Rubric," which the Council thereupon engrafted upon the book, to explain the meaning of the posture, was probably not of Cranmer's penning, and seems to have had no sanction from Cranmer. 1

It was not with a view to the Prayerbook only that Cranmer desired the help of the leading foreign divines: he was anxious to renew under Edward what had fallen through under Henry, the attempt to formulate some general Confession of Faith which might be accepted by all reformed Christians, so as to present an unbroken front to Rome,—and not to Rome only. " Although all controversies cannot be settled in this world," he wrote to Melanchthon, "because the party opposed to the truth will not assent to the Church's judgment, yet it is desirable that the members of the true Church should come to an agreement concerning the principal articles of Church teaching." 2 When he found that this scheme was doomed to failure, he communicated to the foreigners his determination to draw up a separate Confession for the English Church, and received the

> 1 See the curious history in Dixon iii. 475 foil.
> 2 Jenkyns i. 348. Dated March 27, 1552.

encouragement of Calvin. 1 He had already for some time past used certain articles as a test for all preachers and lecturers whom he licensed. 2 In the last year of Edward's reign, he succeeded in procuring that Forty-two Articles should be set forth and put in general use, though not by order of Convocation. They were founded upon that adaptation of the Confession of Augsburg which, in the reign of Henry, Cranmer had devised with the deputation from Germany with a view to doctrinal unity. Although these Articles were frequently examined and emended by the Council, and by experts, they were, no doubt, mainly the Archbishop's work, and they are the foundation of our present Thirty-nine. No hard and narrow dogmatism was in them opposed to the dogmatisms of the Continent. " They showed," says Mr. Dixon, " a surprisingly comprehensive and moderate spirit. The broad soft touch of Cranmer lay upon them." 3

Another of Cranmer's labours was destined to have less effect upon the Church than his labours for the Prayerbook and the Articles. Ever since the Submission of the Clergy, in the time of Warham, ecclesiastical discipline, as such, had been in abeyance. No one knew what parts of the old Canon Law were still in force, nor what ecclesiastical tribunals were empowered to do. By the Act of Submission the revision of the ecclesiastical law was entrusted to a commission of thirty-two persons, to be nominated by the Crown. From time to time the commission was indeed nominated, but it never did any work. Probably Henry VIII. had no wish to see a new code established which

> 1 See Jenkyns i. 347. 2 See above, p. 139.
> 3 Dixon iii. 520.

might define and restrict his powers over the Church. Archbishop Cranmer, however, made repeated efforts to rectify this chaotic state of things. The last of these efforts issued—the date is uncertain, but it was in Edward's reign—in the production of the book called the Reformatio Legum Ecclesiasticarum. It \vas not the unaided composition of the Archbishop. Peter Martyr seems to have had some share in it, and it took its literary form—in the Latin—from the hand of Walter Haddon. Yet the conception of the work was Cranmer's, and it is to be presumed that its proposed enactments indicate what Cranmer, under the influence of his foreign counsellors, was prepared to defend.

The form of the book is that of a series of royal enactments. The King commences with declaring himself the minister of God, and desiring and commanding that all his subjects should embrace and profess the Christian religion. Those who refuse it, estrange God from themselves; and the King pronounces their property and their life to be forfeited. The true foundation for a religious system of law is said to lie in a right belief; and accordingly the first part of the book consists of a statement of the Catholic rule of faith, to which is subjoined a description of various heresies with which the Church is threatened. These heresies include the chief heresies of ancient times; but the main censures of the book are directed against Popish doctrines on the one hand, and still more emphatically against the Anabaptist doctrines on the other. Nor was the threat of death for heresy intended to be but a Irutum fulmen. Joan Bocher was not the only person burned for heresy under Edward VI., and Cranmer himself sat on the commission which sent to the stake a Flemish impugner of the Divinity of Christ. 1

There is, of course, much difference between the sacramental teaching in the Reformatio Legum and that of the Necessary Erudition. " We will," the King is made to say, " that the symbolical bread and wine, if not used for the pious and scriptural purpose of Communion, should be held in no higher esteem than the bread and wine which we daily use." The Lutheran doctrine of the Eucharist is described as being no less of a quagmire than the Roman. Men are warned against supposing that regenerative force and spiritual grace reside in the baptismal font itself. Yet the orthodoxy of Cranmer condemns severely the opposite error of the Sacramentarians,—as in that age they were called. " Great is the rashness of those who reduce the sacraments to bare signs and outward badges by which the religion of Christians may be known from that of others, and who consider not how great wickedness it is to conceive of these holy ordinances of God as though they were empty and hollow things." It is "a cruel impiety" which refuses Baptism to little children. "The children of Christians belong to God and the

Church," as much as those of the Hebrews, who received circumcision in infancy. It is, however, an impious and superstitious thing to hold that the grace of God is so tied to the sacraments that children dying unbaptized, through no fault of their own, are lost:—" We judge," says the King, " that the truth is far otherwise." 2

There are things in the book which show that Cranmer had parted with other of his earlier convictions besides those which concerned the Eucharist. He who had so 1 Dixon iii. 273. 2 Pp. 16, 18, 19 (ed. 1850).

sharply reprobated the German Reformers for allowing divorce, now recommended that if one of the parties to a marriage was guilty of adultery, the other, being blameless, should be permitted to form a new alliance. This was grounded upon the assumption that our Lord's words, " saving for the cause of fornication," meant the sin of adultery, and applied to the c: marrying another," as well as to the " putting away " of the first partner. Desertion, long absence, deadly enmity, ill-usage, were also considered sufficient to warrant divorce. A strong condemnation was pronounced upon the separations vinculo durante, which had formerly been permitted.

Perhaps no part of the work is more revolutionary than that which dealt with the constitutional action of the Church at large. If a bishop, after paternal admonition, proved negligent in the maintenance of discipline, it was provided that the archbishop should have power to put another man in his place. No reference is made to the time-honoured Convocations of the English provinces:—whether they were to be considered as abrogated, or whether they were to remain as an engine for the taxation of the clergy and the like, may be uncertain; but they are not mentioned. Instead of them, or possibly alongside of them, the archbishop of each province is at liberty to summon, with the royal approval, a synod of his provincial bishops, and of them only, for the determination of any grave question that may arise. In each diocese a yearly synod is to be held, before Palm Sunday, which is to be attended by all the clergy of the diocese. Laymen who receive the special permission of the bishop may be present at the deliberations; the rest are excluded. At the close of the deliberations, the bishop may

pronounce canons and decrees of binding validity. The benefits of such synods are set forth in just and striking terms, and especially the benefit of direct intercourse between the bishop and his clergy. " By means of such synods union and love between the bishop and clergy will be increased and maintained. The bishop will form closer acquaintance with his clergy, and will address them; while the clergy will hear the bishop speaking face to face with them, and will be able, when necessary, to put questions to him." 1

The duties of patrons are very impressively set forth; and the bishop is directed to form a body of examiners, whose business it shall be, along with the archdeacon, and (when possible) with the bishop himself, to examine every man presented 'to a living, and not to institute him if the examination is unsatisfactory. Before the examination, the candidate is to be put on his oath to answer faithfully. Then strict inquiry is to be made, both with regard to his principles of life, and with regard to his "views of the Catholic faith and the sacred mystery of the Trinity," of the canonical Scriptures, and of current controversies. The examiners are then to hear him expound the Catechism. Infirmities such as blindness, stammering, hideous disfigurement, bad breath, are to preclude a man from holding a benefice. 2

It is always a hard thing to draw up a paper constitution ; and most of all in the case of a society like the Church, in which tradition must necessarily count for much. The Reformatio Legum was of such a character. Instead of selecting from the mass of existing canons those which were deemed to be still useful 1 P. 108 foil. 2 P. 59 foil.

for the guidance of the Church of England, and adding to them such new ones as experience suggested, it proceeded tabula rasa to provide for every contingency of Church life in an entirely new form. It is on the whole a good thing for the Church of England that the project never became law, either in Edward's time, or later, when Parker revived it under Elizabeth. Yet the work was a bold and honest attempt to remedy a great evil, and to simplify ecclesiastical law; and the greater part of the book is admirable for its wisdom and its high spiritual tone.

The wisest and most spiritual reforms in religion do not always carry the consent and goodwill of the people whom they are intended to benefit, and it was the misfortune of Archbishop Cranmer to be often on the unpopular side, even in the reign of Edward. The introduction of the first English Prayerbook was the signal for a formidable insurrection in the west country, as the overthrow of the monasteries had been the signal for the Pilgrimage of Grace in the north. While Russell and Grey of Wilton were mowing down the men of Devon and Cornwall with the swords and muskets of foreign mercenaries, the Archbishop was set to demolish with his pen the demands which they sent in to the Council. It is an essay which calls forth varied feelings in the reader. While with some biographers of Cranmer we may admire the ease and homeliness of the style, with others we may wonder at the way in which Cranmer mixes learned arguments with contemptuous chiding of the ignorant west countrymen. " O ignorant men of Devonshire and Cornwall," he exclaims, "as soon as ever I heard your articles, I thought that you were deceived by some crafty papists,

to make you ask you wist not what. How many of you, I pray you, do know certainly which be called the General Councils, and holy decrees of the fathers, and what is in them contained ? The holy decrees, as they call them, be nothing else but the laws and ordinances of the Bishop of Rome, whereof the most part be made for his own advancement, glory, and lucre. A great number of the Councils repugn one against another; how should they then be all kept, when one is contrary to another, and the keeping of one is the breaking of another ?" These statements the Archbishop proceeds to illustrate with copious examples; and the contradictions become more pointed when he discusses the second demand, that along with all the decrees of the General Councils the Six Articles should be put in force again. "It is contained," he says, "in the Canons of the Apostles that a priest under no pretence of holiness may put away his wife; and if he do, he shall be excommunicated. And the Six Articles say that if a priest put not away his wife, he shall be taken for a felon. You be cunning men, if you can set these two together."

" Will you not understand what the priest prayeth for you ? Had you rather be like pies or parrots, that be taught to speak and yet understand not one word what they say, than be true

Christian men, that pray unto God in heart and faith ? I have heard suitors murmur at the bar, because their attornies have pleaded theircases in the French tongue, which they understood not. Why then be you offended that the priests, which pleadeth your cause before God, should speak such language as you may understand ? Be you such enemies to your own country that you will not suffer us

to laud God, to thank Him, and to use His sacraments in our own tongue ? "

"You will have neither man nor woman communicate with the priest. Alas, good simple souls, how be you blinded with the papists! The very words of the Mass show plainly that it was ordained not only for the priest, but for others also to communicate with the priest. For in the very Canon which they so much extol, and which is so holy that no man may know what it is, and therefore is read so softly that no man can hear it, in that same Canon, I say, is a prayer containing this ; that ' not only the priest, but as many beside as communicate with him, may be fulfilled with grace and heavenly benediction.' And although I would exhort every good Christian man often to receive the Holy Communion, yet I do not recite these things to the intent that the old Canons should be restored again, which commanded every man present to receive the Communion with the priest; which Canons, if they were now used, I fear that many would receive it unworthily; but I speak them to condemn your article, which would have nobody to be communicated with the priest. Which your article condemneth the old decrees, canons, and General Councils,—condemneth all the old primitive Church, all the old ancient holy doctors and martyrs, and all the forms and manner of masses that were ever made, both new and old. Therefore eat again this article, if you will not be condemned of the whole world."

" Is this the holy Catholic faith, that the Sacrament should be hanged over the altar and worshipped ? Innocent III., about 1215 years after Christ, did ordain that the Sacrament should be kept under lock and key.

After him came Honorius III.; and although this Honorius added the worshipping of the Sacrament, yet he made no mention of the hanging thereof over the high altar; and in Italy it is not yet used until this day. And will you have all them that will not consent to your article to die like heretics that hold against the Catholic faith ?"

" A most godly prince of famous memory, King Henry VIII., pitying to see his subjects many years brought up in darkness and ignorance of God by the erroneous doctrine and traditions of the Bishop of Rome, with the counsel of all his nobles and learned men, studied by all means, and that to his no little danger and charges, to bring you out of your said ignorance and darkness. And our most dread Sovereign Lord that now is, succeeding his father as well in this godly intent as in his realms and dominions, hath with no less care and diligence studied to perform his father's purpose. And you, like men that wilfully shutteth their own eyes, refuse to receive the light. You will have the Sacrament of the Altar delivered to the lay people but once in the year, and then but under one kind. What injury do you to many godly persons! In the Apostles' time, the people of Jerusalem received it every day. And after, they received it in some places every day, in some places four times in the week, in some places three times, some twice, and commonly everywhere at the least once in the week. In the beginning, when men were most godly and most fervent in the Holy Spirit, then they received the Communion daily. But when the Spirit of God began to be more cold in men's hearts, and they waxed more worldly than godly, then their desire was not so hot to receive the

Communion as it was before. An ungodly man abhorreth it, and not without cause dare in no wise approach thereunto. But to them that live godly, it is the greatest comfort that in this world can be imagined; and the more godly a man is, the more sweetness and spiritual pleasure and desire he shall have often to receive it. And will you be so ungodly to command the priest that he shall not deliver it to him but at Easter, and then but only in one kind?"

" O superstition and idolatry! how they prevail among you ! The very true heavenly bread, the food of everlasting life, offered unto you in the sacrament of the Holy Communion, you refuse to eat but only at Easter; and the cup of the most holy Blood, wherewith you were redeemed and washed from your sins, you refuse utterly to drink of at any time. And yet in the stead of these you will eat often of the unsavoury and poisoned bread of the Bishop of Rome, and drink of his stinking puddles, which he nameth holy bread and holy water!"

" You say that you will have the old service, because the new is ' like a Christmas game You declare yourselves what spirit you be led withal, or rather what spirit leadeth them that persuaded you that the word of God is but like a Christmas game. It is more like a game and a fond play to hear the priest speak aloud to the people in Latin, and the people listen with their ears to hear, and some walking up and down in the church saying other prayers in Latin, and none understandeth other. Forasmuch as you understood not the old Latin service, I shall rehearse some things in English which were wont to be read in Latin, that when you understand them you may judge them,

whether they or God's word seem to be more like plays or Christmas games." This the Archbishop proceeds to do, in very plain English indeed. " In the English service is there nothing else but the eternal word of God. St. Paul saith plainly that the word of God is foolishness only to them that perish; but to them that shall be saved it is God's might and power. To some it is a lively savour unto life, and to some it is a deadly savour unto death. If it be to you but a Christmas game, it is then a savour of death unto death. But as Christ commonly excused the simple people, because of their ignorance, and justly condemned the scribes and Pharisees which by their crafty persuasions led the people out of the right way, so I think not you so much to be blamed as these Pharisees and papistical priests which, abusing your simplicity, caused you to ask you wist not what."

" To reason with you by learning which be unlearned, it were but folly. The Scripture maketh mention of two places where the dead be received after this life, of Heaven and of Hell; but of Purgatory is not one word spoken. Purgatory was wont to be called a fire as hot as Hell, but not so long during. But now the defenders of Purgatory within this realm be ashamed so to say: nevertheless they say it is a third place, but where or what it is, they confess themselves they cannot tell. Truth it is that Scripture maketh mention of Paradise and Abraham's bosom after this life; but these be places of joy and consolation, not of pains and torments. Seeing that the Scriptures so often and so diligently teach us to relieve all them that be in necessity, to feed the hungry, to clothe the naked, and so to all other that have need of our help; and the same in no place

maketh mention either of such pains in Purgatory, or what comfort we may do them; it is certain that the same is feigned for lucre, and not grounded upon God's word."

For the rest it will be observed what terrific reality Cranmer's loyal Erastianism gave to St. Paul's saying, that those who resist authority receive to themselves damnation. "This I assure you of, that if all the whole world should pray for you until doomsday, their prayers should no more avail for you than they should avail the devils in hell, if they prayed for them, unless you be penitent and sorry for your disobedience." 1

Notwithstanding the severity of this document, the Archbishop's behaviour towards Papists became more and more lenient as he receded 'further and further from them in opinion. The vicar of Stepney, formerly Abbot of St. Mary of Grace, was brought before him one day at

Croydon for having the bells rung while the licensed preachers were preaching in his church. The Archbishop, says the prosecutor, " was too full of lenity: a little he rebuked him, and bade him do no more so. ' My Lord,' said I, ' methinks you are too gentle unto so stout a papist.' ' Well,' said he, ' we have no law to punish them by.' ' We have, my Lord/ said I; ' if I had your authority, I would be so bold to unvicar him, or minister some sharp punishment unto him and such other. If ever it come to their turn, they will show you no such favour.' ' Well,' said he, ' if God so provide, we must abide it.' ' Surely,' said I, * God will never con you thank for this, but rather take the sword from such as will not use it upon His enemies.' And

1 Jenkyns ii. 202 foil. The above are, of course, but brief samples from the whole document.

thus we departed." 1 "He always bare a good face and countenance unto the papists," says Morice, "and would both in word and deed do very much for them, pardoning their offences; and on the other side, somewhat over severe against the protestants. On a time, a friend of his declared unto him that he therein did very much harm; whereunto he made this answer, and said—' What will ye have a man do to him that is not yet come to the knowledge of the truth of the Gospel ? Shall we perhaps, in his journey coming towards us, by severity and cruel behaviour overthrow him, and as it were in his voyage stop him ? I take not this the way to allure men to embrace the doctrine of the Gospel.'"

Nor was it only private zealots who took offence at Cranmer's ways. Towards the end of Edward's reign he was sadly out of favour with the leading spirits on the Council. " I have heard," says Bidley, " that Cran-mer, and another whom I will not name, were both in high displeasure, but especially Cranmer, for repugning as they might against the late spoil of the church goods, taken away only by commandment of the higher powers, without any law or order of justice, and without any request or consent of those to whom they did belong." 3 " I would to God," wrote Northumberland to Cecil, "it might please the King's Majesty to appoint Mr. Knox to the office of Rochester bishopric. He would be a whetstone to quicken and sharp the Bishop of Canterbury; whereof he had need." 4 When he attempted to gain legal sanction for his new code of Church Law, Northumberland turned fiercely upon him, and abused him—this time for the outspokenness of

1 Narratives of the Reformation p. 157.
2 Ibid. p. 246. 3 D ixon jii. 486> 4 Ibid , ai 45L

the licensed preachers. " You bishops," he said, " look to it at your peril that the like happen not again, or you and your preachers shall suffer for it together." l Cranmer was convinced that the Duke had been " seeking long time his destruction." 2 Even the young Cecil, who afterwards learned to speak very differently of him, took it upon him to task Cranmer for covetous-ness—presumably in not alienating his revenues to the courtiers fast enough. To all, he answered meekly. " As for your admonition," he wrote to Cecil, " I take it most thankfully, as I have ever been most glad to be admonished by my friends. But as for the saying of St. Paul, Qui volunt ditescere, incidunt in tentationem, I fear it not half so much as I do stark beggary. I have more care to live now as an Archbishop, than I had to live like a scholar of Cambridge." 3

Accusations like those of Cecil had indeed been brought against the Archbishop in the days of Henry. Men who coveted the endowments of his see " found means to put it into the King's head that the Archbishop of Canterbury kept no hospitality correspondent unto his revenues and dignity, but sold his woods, and by great incomes and fines maketh money to purchase lands for his wife and his children. The King hearing this tale, and something smelling what they went about," says Morice, " left off any farther to talk of that matter. Notwithstanding, within a month after, whether it was of chance or of purpose it is unknown, the King, going to dinner, called Mr. Seymour unto him, 4 and said, ' Go ye straightways unto Lambeth, and

1 Dixon iii. 512. 2 Jenkyns i. 362.

3 Ibid, i. 351.

4 The King's brother-in-law, who was the chief complainant.

bid my Lord of Canterbury come and speak with me, at two of the clock at afternoon.' Incontinently Mr. Seymour came to Lambeth, and being brought into the hall by the porter, it chanced the hall was set to dinner; and when he was at the screen, and perceived the hall furnished with three principal messes, besides the rest of the tables thoroughly set, having a guilty conscience of his untrue report made to the King, recoiled back, and would have gone in to my Lord by the chapel way. Mr. Nevile, being steward, brought him back unto my Lord throughout the hall; and when he came to my Lord and had done his message, my Lord caused him to sit down and dine with him." On Seymour's return, the King asked whether my Lord had dined before Seymour came. "No forsooth (said Mr. Seymour), for I found him at dinner." "Well (said the King), what cheer made he you ?" " With these words, Mr. Seymour kneeled down and besought the King's Maj esty of pardon. ' What is the matter ?' said the King. ' I perceive,' said Mr. Seymour, ' that I did abuse your Highness with an untruth; for besides your Grace's house, I think he be not in the realm, of none estate or degree, that hath such a hall furnished, or that fareth more honourably at his own table.'" The incident was in Morice's opinion the means of averting a wholesale alienation of ecclesiastical property. 1

More and more towards the end of Edward's reign, Cranmer retired into private life, and to the care of his diocese. Morice and Foxe between them supply us with a fairly full description of the Archbishop at home. " Concerning his behaviour towards his family," says his

1 Morice p. 260. foil. Morice elaborately refutes the charge that Cranmer had impoverished his see.

secretary, " I think there was never such a master amongst men, both feared and entirely beloved; for as he was a man of most gentle nature, void of all crabbed and churlish conditions, so he could abide no such qualities in any of his servants. But if any such outrageousness were in any of his men or family, the correction of those enormities he always left to the ordering of his officers, who weekly kept a counting-house. And if anything universally were to be reformed or talked of on that day, which commonly was Friday, the same was put to admonition. And if it were a fault of any particular man, he was called forth before the company, to whom warning was given, that if he so used himself after three monitions he should lose his service. And surely there was never any committed to the porter's lodge unless it were for shedding of blood, picking, or stealing." 1

" This worthy man," says Foxe, who probably derived the information from Morice, "evermore gave himself to continual study, not breaking that order that he in the University commonly used; that is, by five of the clock in the morning at his book, and so consuming the time in study and prayer until nine of the clock. He then applied himself (if the Prince's affairs did not call him away) until dinner-time to hear suitors, and to dispatch such matters as appertained unto his special cure and charge; which principally consisted in reformation of corrupt religion and in setting forth of true and sincere doctrine. For the most part always being in commission he associated himself with learned men for sifting and bolting out of one matter or another, for

1 Morice p. 269.

the commodity and profit of the Church of England. 1 By means whereof, and what for his private study, he was never idle; besides that, he accounted it no idle point to bestow one hour or twain of the day in reading over such works and books as daily came from beyond the seas. After dinner, having no suitors, for an hour or thereabouts he would play at the chess, or behold such as could play. That done, then again to his ordinary study (at the which commonly he for the most part stood, and seldom sat), and there continuing until five of the clock, bestowed that hour in hearing the Common Prayer, and walking or using some honest pastime until supper time. At supper, if he had no appetite (as many times he would not sup), yet would he sit down at the table, having his ordinary provision of his mess furnished with expedient company, he wearing on his hands his gloves, because he would (as it were) thereby wean himself from eating of meat, but yet keeping the company with such fruitful talk as did repask and much delight the hearers, so that by this means hospitality was well furnished, and the alms chest well maintained for relief of the poor. After supper, he would consume one hour at the least in walking or some other honest pastime, and then again until nine of the clock at one kind of study or another." 2

1 " Specially having almost twenty years together learned men continually sitting with him in commission for the trying out and setting forth of the religion received, and for the discussing of other matters in controversy, some of them daily at diet with him, and some ever more lying in his house." (Morice p. 267.)

2 Foxe viii. 13.

CHAPTER V CRANMER'S LAST YEARS

As the death of Edward approached, Archbishop Cranmer allowed himself to be persuaded into joining the plot of the young King and Northumberland to divert the succession to the throne. Elizabeth, no less than Mary, was excluded by that plot, which to a certain extent relieves those who took part in it from having been governed by theological prepossessions. It ought also to be remembered that at the time of Edward's death the title of Mary and Elizabeth was by no means free from uncertainty. Parliament had, it is true, permitted Henry VIII. to determine the succession by will, and in his will he had named Mary and Elizabeth next after Edward. But both of them were still, by Act of Parliament, illegitimate. Not until after Mary's coronation did the obsequious Parliament annul its own act which had declared her illegitimate, laying •all the blame of that act on Cranmer. And it might well be argued—as in fact the Judges affirmed—that if Henry had a right to bequeath the crown like a private property, Edward possessed the same right. There was no great moral fault in consenting to the proposed arrangement.

Nevertheless it was a grievous mistake, and a man 165
of more independence of mind would not have made it. For Cranmer was convinced at the time that it was a wrong policy. His was the last signature appended to the unlucky document, and he fought hard against signing. He earnestly endeavoured to obtain an interview with the King, his godson; but it was not allowed, except in the presence of two of Northumberland's partisans. " I desired," he writes to Mary, " to talk with the King's Majesty alone, but I could not be suffered, and so I failed of my purpose. For if I might have communed with the King alone, and at good leisure, my trust was that I should have altered him from that purpose; but they being present, my labour was in vain. That will, God, He knoweth, I never liked; nor never anything grieved me so much that your Grace's brother did." But all the rest of the Privy Council had signed; and all the judges and law officers of the Crown, but one, gave it as their opinion that the King had power to make such a will; and the dying boy pressed the Archbishop hard. " Being the sentence of the Judges," he writes, " methought it became not me, being unlearned in the law, to stand against my Prince therein. And so at length I was required by

the King's Majesty himself to set to my hand to his will; saying that he trusted that I alone would not be more repugnant to his will than the rest of the Council were (which words surely grieved my heart very sore), and so I granted him to subscribe his will, and to follow the same. For the which I submit myself most humbly unto your Majesty, acknowledging mine offence with most grievous and sorrowful heart, and beseeching your mercy and pardon; which my heart giveth me shall not be denied unto me, being

granted before to so many, which travailed not so much to dissuade both the King and his Council as I did." x

In thus begging for his life, the Archbishop had no intention of begging to retain his place. He knew too well the line which Mary was likely to take, to suppose that he could remain Archbishop. He sought for no renewal of his license, as at the accession of Edward. He only asked that before quitting his office he might have some conversation with the Queen. " I will never, God willing," he wrote, " be author of sedition, to move subjects from the obedience of their heads and rulers; which is an offence most detestable. If I have uttered my mind to your Majesty, being a Christian Queen and Governor of the realm (of whom I am most assuredly persuaded, that your gracious intent is, above all other regards, to prefer God's true word, His honour and glory)—if I have uttered, I say, my mind unto your Majesty, then I shall think myself discharged. For it lieth not in me, but in your Grace only, to see the reformation of things that be amiss. To private subjects it appertaineth not to reform things, but quietly to suffer that they cannot amend. Yet nevertheless to show your Majesty my mind in things appertaining to God, methink it my duty, knowing that I do, and considering the place which in times past I have occupied." ' Cranmer's theory of the relation between kings and primates may have been incorrect, but it was at least consistent. His Erastianism rose to the height of a great spiritual principle.

To do Mary justice, she was disposed to deal most leniently with all who were concerned in the abortive plot. It was with the utmost reluctance that she consented to proceed against the poor girl who for a few hours had been thrust into her throne. Cecil, afterwards Lord Burghley, who had been more compromised than Cranmer, remained notwithstanding a member of her Council. Cranmer himself was left at liberty. Perhaps it was hoped that he would have fled from the country, as scores of others were now doing. Archbishop Heath is reported to have said that there was a design of pensioning him off, and allowing him to retire into private life. [1]

But Providence had destined for him a more distinguished ending to his career. He paid a visit to the Court one day—it seems to have been for the generous purpose of befriending Sir John Cheke, who was involved in the same trouble as himself. [2] About the same date, his suffragan, Thornden, Bishop of Dover, who owed so much to the Archbishop, took upon him to say the Latin Mass in Canterbury Cathedral. The rumour got about that he had done so by Cranmer's orders, and that Cranmer himself had offered to say Mass before the Queen. This rumour roused him—him who was so little angered at any merely personal calumnies—to a flame of indignation. Worldly prudence—all solicitude for his own safety—was flung to the winds. He wrote a declaration, which it was his intention to have sealed with his archiepis-copal seal and affixed to the doors of St. Paul's and of all the churches in the City, fiercely repudiating the slander. "Although I have been well exercised these twenty years to suffer and bear evil reports and lies, and have not been much grieved thereat, but have borne all things quietly; yet untrue reports to the hindrance of God's truth are in no wise to be tolerated and suffered. Wherefore these be to signify to the world, that it was not I that did set up the Mass at Canterbury, but it was a false, flattering, lying, and dissimuling monk which caused Mass to be set up there, without mine advice or counsel. Reddat illi Dominus in die illo" He ended by offering to prove that the Prayerbook, and all the doctrine and religion set out by the late King, was more pure and scriptural than any other doctrine that had been used in England for a thousand years. [1] It was still illegal to use the Latin Mass in the Church of England, and the English service was the only authorised service in the country. It might have been thought no crime to offer to speak in defence of it. But Cranmer was at once committed to the Tower, on the charge of his treason against Mary, and of aggravating the same by spreading about seditious bills. [2] "This day," wrote Bishop Bonner a few days later to his agents, " is looked Mr. Canterbury must be placed where is meet for him. He is become very humble," he adds, putting his own construction upon the Primate's meekness, " and ready to submit himself to all things; but that will not serve." [3]

Two months later, Cranmer was tried at the Guildhall, with the Lady Jane and others. He pleaded guilty, and was condemned. In the Tower he remained, however, from his condemnation in November 1553, till the

[1] Jenkyns iv. 2.

[2] Foxe says that before his attainder he took pains to pay every penny that he owed to any one, so that he might be "his. own man " (viii. 14).

[3] Dixon iv. 38. Bonner had indeed some excuse for speaking triumphantly. He had been very badly treated in the previous reign ; and Cranmer himself had behaved ill towards him ; see Dixon iii. 133 foil.

following April. He does not seem to have been expressly pardoned for his treason, but no more was said about it. There was a charge to be brought against him which was of far greater importance in the Queen's eyes. It was the charge of heresy.

There were reasons, if Mary had only known of them— perhaps she did not—why Mary should have been especially careful to protect the Archbishop. If it had not been for his interference in earlier days, Mary would have lost her liberty, if not her life. Soon after the birth of Elizabeth, Henry VIII. had been highly incensed against his elder daughter for refusing to abandon the title of Princess, which she had formerly worn. He fully purposed, says Morice, to send her to the Tower, " and there to suffer as a subject, because she would not obey unto the laws of the realm in refusing the Bishop of Home's authority and religion." Cranmer, who had laboured so earnestly and in vain to save other victims of the Act of Succession, interposed more successfully on Mary's behalf. The King granted his generous request, but told him that one of them would some day see cause to repent of the decision. 1 But no personal feelings of obligation would have availed to make Mary forgive Cranmer after his late proclamation. To men who were willing to espouse her religious policy she could forgive anything. Gardiner had been at least as forward as Cranmer in the matter of her mother's divorce, and so far as we know had made no efforts on behalf of the adherents of Catherine and of the Pope. But he had suffered under Edward, and had conformed under Mary, and she found it easy to make him Lord Chancellor of England, and to put herself under his 1 Narratives of the Reformation p. 259.

political guidance. All his offences were forgotten; and so might Cranmer's have been, could he have changed his religious ground. But he could not. He was in the Queen's eyes a heretic, and she meant him to die a heretic's death.

According to all the laws of Catholic Christendom no bishop can be tried on such a charge as heresy except by men of his own order. But the Convocation which sat in the beginning of 1554, deputed eight members of the Lower House, none of whom was more than a presbyter, to examine the Archbishop, together with Bishops Latimer and Ridley. There was as yet no law of the land by which they could be condemned; but when this was objected, Weston, the Prolocutor of the Lower House, and head of the deputed members, replied—" It forceth not for a law; we have commission to proceed with them; when they be dispatched let their friends sue the law." 1 The illegality was not worse than many things done by commission in the two previous reigns; but it was not a hopeful presage for the returning Catholicism of England. The three prelates were removed from the Tower, where of late they had been imprisoned in one chamber, and had spent their time in studying the New Testament together. They were conveyed to Oxford, where the delegates of Convocation were met and reinforced by representatives of the two Universities.

The proceedings resembled those in which Cranmer had taken his part under Henry, when the form of a judicial investigation was exchanged for that of an academic debate. No evidence was called to ascertain what Cranmer and the others had taught. The authorities 1 Dixon iv. 176.

professed to doubt, and perhaps Cranmer's history gave them some reason to doubt, whether his heresy was more than a passing phase of opinion, which he might be brought by argument to surrender. 1 Certain articles concerning the Eucharist had been agreed upon which the doctors were to maintain, and Cranmer was to accept or to contest them. The simple and unself-asserting man made no objection either to the composition of the Court, or to the method to be employed. On Saturday, April 14, he was brought by the Mayor of Oxford into the choir of St. Mary's, where the commissioners were seated before the altar. He "reverenced them with much humility, and stood with his staff in his hand; and notwithstanding having a stool offered him he refused to sit." Weston commenced the proceedings with a short oration in praise of unity, in the course of which he traced Cranmer's career, and said how he had fallen away from the unity of the Church, and now the Queen desired them to bring him back to it, if they could. Cranmer replied that he " was very glad to come to a unity, so that it were in Christ, and agreeable to His holy word." The three articles were then read out. The first of them affirmed that " the natural body of Christ" was in the sacrament. Cranmer " did read them over three or four times," and then asked what they meant by " natural." " Do you not mean," saith he, " corpus organicum ? "—a body with its different members and complete structure. Some answered one thing, and some another; but the general answer was, " the same that was born of the Virgin." " Then the

1 Bishop Cranmer's Recantacyons p. 17: Principio, quia de gravitate valetudinis dubitabatur, anceps etiam curatio prwscripta est, quasi tentandi vulneris causa.

Bishop of Canterbury denied it utterly," and said that he " would not agree in that unity with them." He was sent back to the gaol, with the intimation that he was to send in his opinion that night in writing, and that he would be called upon to dispute on the Monday. Any books which he desired were to be given him. The modesty of his behaviour is said to have brought tears to the eyes of some of his opponents. 1

On the Monday, at eight o'clock, they met again. Westoa laid down at the outset that it was not lawful to question the truth of the three articles. The Archbishop replied that it was vain to dispute on points which it was not lawful to question. Nevertheless, he prepared himself to dispute. He had been well accustomed to exercises of the kind at Cambridge, and was an extremely skilful debater. Sir Thomas More had confessed himself staggered by the subtlety of his arguments. Bishop Gardiner had declared that Cran-mer overcame him by his ingenious sophistry. On this occasion he argued in a manner worthy of his reputation. The unsparing foe, who afterwards chronicled his Recantacyons, says that it was observed how Cranmer played a double part in the disputations; he was unable to understand how the two things could be reconciled. On the one hand, he says, Cranmer, true to his own character—and it is a high testimony—would not utter a too eager or a contemptuous expression, but kept tongue and temper under restraint, and every word carried an appearance of modesty and respectfulness; while, on the other hand, he made himself the outspoken representative of Zwinglianism. 2 It is difficult to

1 Foxe vi. 441.
2 Bishop Crammer's Becantacyons p. 19.

imagine how a man, speaking for his life, as Cranmer thought himself to be, could be so calm and even witty. He was accused, for instance, of falsifying St. Hilary by reading in a certain passage vero for vere; and when he replied that, even if vere were the right reading, the change of one letter made little difference, Weston observed that there was some difference between pastor, a bishop, and pistor, a baker. " Let it be so," replied the ready Archbishop; " yet let pistor be either a baker or maker of bread, ye see here the change of a letter, and yet no great difference to be in the sense." l The written " Explication " which Cranmer had sent in, and which he in vain asked to have read aloud in the course of the disputation, is as spiritual and beautiful as anything that he ever wrote.

But in spite of his skill, and in spite of his spirituality, the position which he had adopted on the Eucharist was a difficult one to defend, and difficult as it would have been in any circumstances, it was made more so by the way in which the debate was conducted. There was "such noise and crying out in the school that his mild voice could not be heard." At one point Weston is said to have stretched out his hand and " set on the rude people to cry out at him indoctum, imperi-tum, impudentem" 2 There were too many disputants against Cranmer, all of them eager to show their acute-ness and their learning, and the discussion ran from topic to topic without any order or progress. " I can report," remonstrated the Archbishop to the Privy Council, " that I never knew nor heard of a more confused disputation in all my life. For albeit there was one appointed to dispute against me, yet every man 1 Foxe vi. 461. 2 Ibid. vi. 454.

spake his mind, and brought forth what him liked, without order. And such haste was made, that no answer could be suffered to be given fully to any argument. And in such weighty and large matters there was no remedy but the disputations must needs be ended in one day, which can scantly well be ended in three months." : After nearly six hours of it the Prolocutor abruptly concluded by calling upon the bystanders to cry all together " Vincit veritas, the truth overcometh." 2 Cranmer now demanded, according to the rule of the schools, that another day should be appointed on which he might be the opponent, and they respond. He complained to the Council that this was not granted; 3 but doubtless it was thought to have been granted, when on the following Thursday he was put up to oppose Harps-field, who kept an act for his doctor's degree. Weston began the argument against Harpsfield, and then suddenly pausing in it, invited Cranmer to take his place. After a grave compliment to Weston, the Archbishop asked, " How Christ's body is in the sacrament, according to your determination ? " Harpsfield (who had been made Archdeacon of Canterbury in the place of Cranmer's brother) replied—" He is there in such sort and manner as He may be eaten." " My next question is,"pursued Cranmer, "whether He hath His quantity and qualities, form, figure and such like properties?" Hereupon ensued a wild hubbub. The doctors were furious with him for such a thrust, and one answered one thing and one another. But Cranmer stuck to his question. At last Harpsfield was forced to reply—" He is there as pleaseth Him to be there." " I would be best contented

1 Jenkyns i. 366. 2 Foxe vi. 468.

3 Jenkyns i. 366.

with that answer said the Archbishop, "if that your appointing of a carnal presence had not driven me of necessity to have enquired, for disputation's sake, how you place Him there, since you will have a natural body." Cranrner was here on his own ground, and drove his antagonists from point to point. At last, to protect Harpsfield from utter discomfiture, Weston, who was perhaps ashamed of the manner in which he had acted three days before, interposed respectfully : " Your wonderful gentle behaviour and modesty, good Mr. Dr. Cranmer, is worthy much commendation : and that I may not deprive you of your right and just deserving, I give you most hearty thanks in my own name, and in the name of all my brethren." At which saying all the doctors gently put off their caps. 1

Notwithstanding this courtesy, the day following, the three bishops were together brought before the commissioners, and " sentence read over them, that they were no members of the Church; and therefore they, their fautors and patrons, were condemned as heretics. They were asked whether they would turn or no; and they bade them read on in the name of God, for they were not minded to turn. So they were condemned all three." Then Cranrner answered—"From this your judgment and sentence I appeal to the just judgment of God Almighty, trusting to be present with Him in heaven for whose presence in the altar I am thus condemned." 2

But none of the three was yet to die. Parliament, for one thing, had not, in April 1554, revived its old laws for the burning of heretics, although the Queen was prepared to act as if it had. Home also disapproved

1 Foxe vi. 518. 2 Ibid. vi. 534.

of the way in which an unreconciled Church and Realm behaved as though it had been restored by proper processes. Not until the following February were the fires lighted, by which time the Queen had been married to Philip, Pole had been received into the kingdom as Legate of the Pope, and the Houses of Parliament had knelt to receive from him Rome's absolution. Then, after the English Church and nation had undergone such a humiliation as it had never undergone before, Pole, who was but a deacon himself, issued a commission for the trying of Latimer and Ridley. The condemnation pronounced by a commission which Rome had not commissioned was treated as invalid. The case of Cranmer, a metropolitan who had worn the pall, was held to belong to the Pope himself. Accordingly the King and Queen made humble suit to Paul IV. to try him. Paul thereupon issued a summons to the imprisoned Archbishop [1] to appear within eighty days at Rome, at the same time delegating the trial of the case to the head of the Roman Inquisition. That functionary in turn delegated the matter to Brooks, Bishop of Gloucester, who proceeded to Oxford, and called before him Cranmer as the accused, and the King and Queen of England as the accusers.

On September 12 the Bishop of Gloucester took his seat in St. Mary's Church, on a scaffold above the high altar, with Martin and Story, the proctors of the King and Queen, on lower seats to his right and left. The sacrament was suspended immediately over his head.

[1] About this time Cranmer seems to have been removed from Bocardo to the house of one of the Proctors of the University, and did not return to prison until after his trial before Brooks (Bishop Cranmer's Eecantacyons pp. 27, 36).

Cranmer was sent for. He stood for awhile, until one of the officials called out—"Thomas, Archbishop of Canterbury, appear here and make answer to that shall be laid to thy charge; that is to say for blasphemy, incontinency, and heresy; and make answer here to the Bishop of Gloucester, representing the Pope's person." "Upon this, he being brought more near unto the scaffold, where the foresaid Bishop sat, he first well viewed the place of judgment, and spying where the King and Queen's Majesty's proctors were, putting off his cap, he first, humbly bowing his knee to the ground, made reverence to the one and after to the other. That done, beholding the Bishop in the face, he put on his bonnet again, making no manner of token of obedience towards him at all." To the Bishop's expostulation, he replied that he " did it not for any contempt to his person, which he would have been content to have honoured as well as any of the other, if his commission had come from as good an authority as theirs;" but that he " had once taken a solemn oath never to consent to the admitting of the Bishop of Rome's authority into this realm of England again, and that he had done it advisedly, and meant by God's grace to keep it." [1]

This, indeed, was the main point of the whole business; for though he was examined on many points in his teaching and career, it was the contest with the Pope that chiefly engrossed his mind. When the trial was over, he sent his own report of it, by the hands of Martin and Story, to Queen Mary, and a strangely powerful and outspoken document it is. Those who think of Cranmer as deficient in courage must have forgotten, if they ever read, his declaration against the Mass [1] Foxe viii. 45.

at the beginning of the reign, and the intrepid monition (for such it is) which he now addressed to the deaf ears of the Queen. " Alas," wrote the great plain Englishman, " it cannot but grieve the heart of any natural subject, to be accused of the King and Queen of his own realm, and specially before an outward judge, or by authority coming from any person out of this realm: where the King and Queen, as if they were subjects within their own realm, shall complain and require justice at a stranger's hands against their own subject, being already condemned to death by their own laws; the like whereof, I think, was never seen. I would have wished to have had some meaner adversaries; and I think that death shall not grieve me much more, than to have my most dread and most gracious Sovereign Lord and Lady (to whom under God I do owe all obedience) to be mine accusers in judgment within their own realm, before any stranger and outward power." " The imperial crown and jurisdiction temporal of this realm is taken immediately from God, to be used under Him only, and is subject unto none but to God alone." He showed at length how harmful to the Crown were the claims of the Pope, and added that he did not think these considerations could have been opened in the Parliament House, or such a foreign authority would never have been received again; " and if I," he said, " should allow such authority within the realm, I could not think myself true either to your Highness, or to this my natural country, knowing that I do know. Ignorance, I know, may excuse other men; but he that knoweth how prejudicial and injurious the power and authority, which he challengeth everywhere, is to this realm, and yet will allow the same, I cannot see in

any wise how he can keep his due allegiance, fidelity, and truth." "This that I have spoken," he subjoins, " against the power and authority of the Pope, I have not spoken (I take God to record and judge) for any malice I owe to the Pope's person, whom I know not; but I shall pray to God to give him grace that he may seek above all things to promote God's honour and glory, and not to follow the trade of his predecessors in these latter days. Nor I have not spoken it for fear of punishment, and to avoid the same, thinking it rather an occasion to aggravate than to diminish my trouble; but I have spoken it for my most bounden duty to the Crown, liberties, laws, and customs of this realm of England, but most especially to discharge my conscience in uttering the truth to God's glory, casting away all fear by the comfort which I have in Christ." 1

If this letter was not daring enough, Cranmer followed it up by a second. " I learned by Dr. Martin that at the day of your Majesty's coronation you took an oath of obedience to the Pope of Rome, and the same time you took another oath to this realm, to maintain the laws, liberties, and customs of the same. I beseech your Majesty to expend and weigh the two oaths together, to see how they do agree, and then—to do as your Grace's conscience shall give you; for I am surely persuaded that willingly your Majesty will not offend nor do against your conscience for nothing. But I fear me that there be contradictions in your oaths, and that those which should have informed your Grace thoroughly, did not their duties therein. If your Majesty ponder the two oaths diligently, I think you shall perceive you were deceived; and then your High-1 Jenkyns i. 369 foil.

ness may use the matter as God shall put in your heart." He ended by saying that if her Majesty would give him leave, he would appear at Rome in answer to the Pope's summons, and that he trusted that God should put in his mouth to defend His truth there as well as here. 1

While Pole, the Legate, was engaged in composing elegant philippics in reply, and Brooks' report of the trial was on its way to Rome, where the maniacal Paul IV. in Consistory pronounced Cranmer contumacious, and commanded that he should be degraded and delivered to the secular power, 2 Cranmer was devising an appeal. He contrived to get a letter taken to a doctor of laws in the University, asking his aid in fashioning an appeal from the Pope to a General Council, as Luther had appealed. He said that the time was short, that the thing must be done with the utmost secrecy, that he felt it to be a man's duty to save his life if he could, and that his chief reason for wishing to live was that he might finish, what he had already begun, a new reply to a new rejoinder of Gardiner's on the Eucharist. Almost the very day that Cranmer penned this letter his old antagonist passed beyond the reach of controversy by death. 3

The weeks drifted away, and near the end of the year 1555, some two months after the deaths of Latimer and Ridley, the first signs of a change were observable in Cranmer. It is said that he expressed a wish to see the good and gentle Tunstall, Bishop of Durham.

1 Jenkyns i. 383.
2 Cranmer was burned at Rome in effigy (Bishop Granmer's Recantacyons p. 69).
3 The letter is in Jenkyns i. 385. Gardiner died November 13, 1555.

For Tunstall Cranmer had always felt a high regard. Tunstall, the friend of Erasmus, had conformed to the First Prayerbook of Edward ; and when in the latter part of that reign a bill to deprive him was brought into tbe House of Lords, Cranmer alone, with one lay peer, contended against it. When a little later he was deprived by a commission, Cranmer utterly refused to have anything to do with it. In Henry's days Tunstall had spoken as strongly against the Papacy as Cranmer, or as Gardiner; but now he had submitted. Tunstall had written a book upon the Eucharist, about the same time as Gardiner and (on the whole) taking the same side. That book Cranmer had with him in Bocardo. 1 The aged prelate was unable to take the journey to Oxford; and besides, he added, in words full of significance, so far from his being any help to Cranmer, Cranmer would be confident of creating doubts in him. It came to Pole's ears that Cranmer would be glad to speak with him; but the fastidious Legate preferred to launch his diatribes at the prisoner from afar. England now swarmed with Spanish divines, who took in the distracted Church of this country the place of the Bucers and A Lascos of the reign before. Pole sent one of these, named Soto, to the Archbishop. Cranmer was not much influenced by Soto; but, after a time, he asked to see another of the Spaniards, John de Villa Garcia. This young man—he was not yet thirty—who was soon to be rewarded for his share in Cranmer's downfall by the chair of Regius Professor in which Peter Martyr had sat, before long established a kind of friendship with the prisoner, though Cranmer warmly repelled his arguments. If the bitter writer of Bishop 1 Bishop Cranmer's Recantacyons p. 24.

Cranmer's Recantacyons may be trusted, the influence of the gaoler upon his lonely prisoner was more effectual than the syllogisms of the Dominican. Between them, however, they succeeded. It was on New Year's Eve that de Garcia first visited Cranmer. At the end of January, or thereabout, Cranmer wrote his first short Submission. No right of the Pope was acknowledged in it, but Cranmer fell back on his ancient principle of yielding to the judgment of State authorities.

"Forasmuch," he wrote, "as the King and Queen's Majesties, by consent of their Parliament, have received the Pope's authority within this realm, I am content to submit myself to their laws herein, and to take the Pope for chief head of the Church of England, so far as God's laws, and the laws and customs of this realm will permit."

It was not to the Pope's laws that he submitted, but to those of the King and Queen; and he accepted the Supreme Headship of the Pope with the same careful reservation with which the Church had accepted Henry's twenty-five years before. A few days more, and he had revoked this submission, but soon substituted for it a more unguarded one:—

" I, Thomas Cranmer, doctor in divinity, do submit myself to the Catholic Church of Christ, and to the Pope, Supreme Head of the same Church, and unto the King and the Queen's Majesties, and unto all their laws and ordinances."

Even this was no renuntiation of his belief on the points in dispute, nor certainly any acknowledgment that the Pope was always right. It was an acknowledgment of a power existing de facto, with which Cranmer would no longer contend. This acknowledgment

he did not revoke before the end. It is said that he began to go to chapel, that he attended Mass, that he walked again in the Litany procession, that on Candlemas Day he held a taper, and that he joined in singing a Requiem or a Dirge. 1

The only answer to these advances was a commission from London to two prelates to act upon the] mandate which had now arrived from Rome, and to degrade Cranmer. The two prelates were Bonner and Thirlby. Thirlby, a good and not illiberal man, had conformed to all the changes, from Henry VIII. to Mary, and kept his seat throughout, though he shrank from changing again under Elizabeth. It was probably for this reason that he was selected for the odious task. The task was the more odious because between him and Cranmer, to whom he was indebted for promotion, there had been a warm personal friendship. "Whether it were jewel, plate, instrument, maps, horse, or anything else," says the Archbishop's secretary, " Thirlby had but to admire, and Cranmer would give it him." 2 Before him and Bonner Cranmer was summoned to appear, on St. Valentine's Day, in the Cathedral of Oxford. Even at that moment he was not spared the weariness of hearing declamations and arguments. He was set up aloft upon the rood-screen, while Harpsfield made a recital of his misdeeds. When the orator had finished, Cranmer flung his arms around the great Rood, which had been re-erected there, with its thorn-crowned Figure, crying—" This is the Judge to whom I refer my hap." 3 He was then dragged down and invested with all the habiliments of an archbishop, only made of

1 Bishop Cranmer's Recantacyons p. 63.
2 See Todd ii. 469. 3 Bishvp Cranmer's RecantacyoM p. 70.

canvas and rags, in mockery. When they put on him the chasuble, which he had not worn for four years, he said—" What! I think I shall say Mass," meaning, though ironically, " I suppose I am to do so;" to which one of Bonner's chaplains answered—"Yes, my Lord; I trust to see you say Mass for all this." " Do you so ? " said Cranmer; " that shall you never see." His submissions thus far had not involved a change of mind on that point. Yet the opinions of Cranmer on the subject were now, if they ever were otherwise, as tolerant as those of Frith had been. The doctors fell to disputing with him about it. "Do you think/' said de Villa Garcia, "that all the Saints are lost, who never heard of your new faith ?" " Nay," replied Cranmer, " I think that you may gain eternal salvation by your faith, and I by mine." " Then," cried the friar, " there is no one faith, from which it is infidelity to differ." The Archbishop acknowledged that in necessary things there was one faith, but not in all. 1 After an oration by Bonner, so insolent in its triumph that Bishop Thirlby " divers times pulled him by the sleeve to make an end," they proceeded to strip him of his insignia, piece by piece. They began with his crosier-staff ; but Cranmer held fast, and refused to deliver it up. Before it could be wrested from him, he plucked oat of his left sleeve a paper, and gave it to them, crying—" I appeal to the next General Council." The paper containing the appeal was put in the hands ot Thirlby, who said respectfully—" My Lord, our commission is to proceed against you omni appellatione remota, and therefore we cannot admit it." "Then you do me the more wrong," answered the prisoner, 1 Bishop Cranmer's Becantacyons p. 72.

rising in his travesty attire above his natural homeliness of temper. " My case is not as every private man's case. The matter is between the Pope and me immediately; and I think no man ought to be a judge in his own cause." " Well," said Thirlby, greatly moved, " if it may be admitted, it shall." When they took away his pall, Cranmer once more flashed with the fire of his great predecessors. " Which of you," he exclaimed, "hath a pall, to take off my pall ?" At last he was stripped of all, his head shaven to obliterate the tonsure, and his fingers scraped where they had once been anointed; they clothed him with a yeoman's gown, and put a townsman's cap upon his head. " Now," said the coarse Bonner, who had no sense of the spiritual tragedy in which he was taking part, "are you no lord any more." 1

The appeal which the Archbishop put in was worthy of its great occasion. He began by protesting that he intended " to speak nothing against one, holy, catholic, and apostolical church, or the authority thereof (the which authority I have in great reverence, and to whom my mind is in all things to obey); and if anything peradventure, either by slipperiness of tongue, or by indignation of abuses, or else by the provocation of mine adversaries, be spoken or done otherwise than well, or not with such reverence as becometh me, I am most ready to amend it." Then, in language which might be taken to imply that he acknowledged the Bishop of Rome to " bear the room of Christ in earth," and to " have authority of God," 2 he affirmed, never-

1 Foxe viii. 79.

2 By the word " although," Cranmer probably meant " even if," like "though " in 1 Cor. xiii. 1.

theless, that the Pope is not thereby "become un-sinnable," and must be resisted if he command anything against the commands of God. Where resistance to him is impossible, because princes, deceived by evil counsel, aid him, there yet lies an appeal from him. " Insomuch that the inferior cannot make laws of not appealing to a superior power, and since it is openly enough confessed that a holy General Council is above the Pope, especially in matters concerning faith, and that he cannot make decrees that men shall not appeal from him to a General Council; therefore I, Thomas Cranmer, Archbishop of Canterbury, or in time past ruler of the Metropolitical Church of Canterbury . . . do challenge and appeal from the Pope, ... as well for myself as for all and every one that cleaveth to me, or will hereafter be on my side, unto a free General Council." It concludes with the noble words: " And I protest and openly confess, that in all my doctrine and preaching, both of the sacrament and of other my doctrine whatsoever it be, not only I mean and judge those things as the Catholic Church and the most holy Fathers of old with one accord have meant and judged; but also I would gladly use the same words that they used and not use any other words, but to set my hand to all and singular their speeches, phrases, ways, and forms of speech which they do use in their treatises upon the sacrament, and to keep still their interpretation. But in this thing I only am accused for an heretic, because I allow not the doctrine lately brought in of the sacrament, and because I consent not to words not accustomed in Scripture and unknown to the ancient Fathers."*

1 Foxe viii. 76. The word "only" belongs, of course, to "this thing," not to " I."

The third and fourth so-called Submissions added nothing to what was contained in the former ones, or indeed in his Appeal itself. In the third, he reaffirmed that he was content to obey the royal ordinances as well concerning the Pope's primacy as others, and promised that he would move and stir all other to do the like. But he referred the judgment of his book on the Sacrament not to the Pope, but to the Catholic Church and to the next General Council. In the fourth, which was signed on February 16, and delivered, like the preceding one, into the hands of the Bishop of London, he only said that he firmly believed in all articles and points of the Christian religion and Catholic faith, as the Catholic Church doth believe, and hath believed from the beginning of Christian religion. He had done nothing so far, that was wholly irreconcileable with his former convictions.

But now, for some reason, although he was informed that his death-warrant was actually signed, there was a change in their treatment of him. A sister of his, who had apparently gone with the Queen's changes, took counsel's opinion whether it was lawful to put an Archbishop to death. 1 At her urgent entreaty he was removed from Bocardo, and lodged in the Deanery of Christ Church; " where/* says the austere martyrolo-gist, " he lacked no delicate fare, played at the bowls, had his pleasure for walking, and all other things that might bring him from Christ." It seemed that he might expect to live. Learned men surrounded him. The Spanish friars plied him incessantly. About the beginning of March Cranmer fell indeed. In a lengthy Latin document, his fifth, no doubt prepared for him 1 Bishop Cranmer's Recantacyons p. 51.

by John de Villa Garcia, in whose presence he copied it out and signed it, Cranmer made a complete recantation of his former convictions upon all the disputed points. He acknowledged the Bishop of Rome as Supreme Head of the visible Church, the Vicar of Christ, whom all were bound to obey. He accepted Transubstantiation, set forth in explicit terms; the six other sacraments as taught by the Church of Rome; the torments of Purgatory, and prayers to the Saints. He expressed penitence for having ever thought differently from the Roman Church, asked the prayers of the faithful that he might be pardoned, and adjured all whom his example or teaching had misled, to return to the unity of the Church. The unhappy man ended by calling God to witness that this profession was not made for any man's fear or favour, but heartily and very gladly.

It was, undoubtedly, a miserable departure from principle ; and yet it is not impossible that an anxiously inquiring man like Cranmer may, in these years of solitary reflexion, and in his recent discussions, have learned sincerely to doubt the rightness of much that had been said and done by him and his associates. A narrow and rigid mind, such as Ridley's or Hooper's, would not have entertained a question of what it had once embraced; but Cranmer was capable of it. With regard to the chief topic in the controversy, it must be remembered that during the greater part of his life Cranmer had been accustomed devoutly to sing his Mass without allowing his traditional belief to be shaken by the Swiss literature which he studied. It was not unnatural if, when Ridley, who had persuaded him to adopt the Zwinglian view, was gone, further thought

and study convinced him that, however loyally he may have intended in his book to follow the Catholic Fathers, he had failed to give due weight to many of their utterances. He had, if I mistake not, really gravitated back towards his earlier position—towards the position of Bishop Tunstall, whom he had asked to see. Finding that he had been wrong on one point, he gave way on all. And then, at his last hour, in that deep self-distrust which was so characteristic of him, he probably felt that he had been unduly swayed by the desire to live, and that it was safest to stand by the opinions which he had formed while he was a free man.

Deeply committed as he now was to the whole Papal system, the fallen Cranmer (no doubt) intended at first to make the best of it; but he was not happy. To the congratulations and offers of Soto he replied, with sobs which choked his utterance, that nothing could be done for him but to implore peace and pardon for him from God, for the pricks of his conscience would give him no rest. His nights were troubled. Alone or in company he repeated the Litanies, with their invocations of the Saints, which in Henry's days he had set aside. As he recited the Penitential Psalms, and came to the words, Fw Thine, arrows stick fast in me, his poor wounded heart sought relief in such a burst of tears, that no one could question the sincerity of his sorrow. He asked for a learned confessor, who might hear and absolve him. Every flitting of his heart was reported to Pole, and to the Queen and Council. Pole granted his request, and Cranmer received absolution from one of the Spanish Dominicans. Many people visited him. He told them how glad he was to be reunited to the flock. Some one brought him back his copy of Sir

Thomas More's Comfort against Tribulation ; and Cran-mer took occasion to say, with truth, that he had never consented to the death of its witty and upright author. The next day he confessed again, and received the Blessed Sacrament, with every expression that might satisfy the demands of those who surrounded him. 1

Had the enemies of the Archbishop been men of wisdom, they would have been contented with the victory which they had gained, and would have suffered the discredited Cranmer to pass out of his prison—for he was in prison again—to a life of contempt. But they were not men of wisdom. They were bent upon a further display of their triumph. There was yet a depth lower for Cranmer to sound; but it is questionable whether it was more base for Cranmer to sign his next document, or for others to give it to him to sign. His sixth Submission made no more complete surrender of principle than the Recantation which preceded it: that would have been impossible. It was only designed for the purpose of making that surrender more abject and more bitter. The man who in February loftily called Christendom to step in and judge between him and the Pope, on March 18 set his hand to sign a fulsome lamentation for having sinned worse than Saul the persecutor and blasphemer, and worse than the crucified robber. He had sinned against heaven, and against the realm of England. He had been the cause and author of the divorce of Henry, and deserved both temporal and eternal punishment for it. Out of that divorce had come the deaths of many good men, the schism of the realm, and havoc beyond imagination. Cranmer said that he had opened the windows to all 1 Bishop Oranmer's Recantacyons p. 78 foil.

the heresies, especially on the sacrament of the Eucharist. It is impossible to doubt who was the author of this tedious Latin exercise. The Scriptural conceits which adorn the composition, and indeed the whole style, and the circumstances, betray the affected hand of Pole, who four days later was to be consecrated to the see of the murdered man.

On March 19, Cranmer's spare time was occupied in sending requests to various Colleges in Oxford—to Christ Church, Magdalen, Corpus Christi, and especially to All Souls, upon which, as Chichele's successor, he made a Founder's claim—that prayers might be offered for him after his 'death,1 and in correcting and signing copies of his recantation. The next day, some more copies were brought to him for the purpose; he signed them, and then said that no one should induce him to sign any more. That evening he received a visit from Cole, the Provost of Eton. Cole's business at Oxford was to preach at Cranmer's burning, and the Queen herself had given him the heads of his discourse. Ever since the beginning of her reign, Mary had been solicitous that " good sermons " should be preached at the burning of heretics. 2 Cole asked Cranmer whether he persevered in the faith, to which he replied that he did. He besought Cole's good offices with Mary on behalf of his orphan son, and wept as he spoke of him. It has been affirmed that Cole never told Cranmer that he was to die; but this appears to have been only a conjecture of Foxe's to account for Cranmer's action afterwards. Cole told the Archbishop that he was charged with the melancholy tidings that he could not be permitted to

1 Bishop Cranmer's Recantacyons pp. 90, 94.
2 Dixon iv. 236.

live. It was a thing so monstrous and unheard of, to put a man to death for an opinion which he had solemnly renounced, that the Archbishop may well have hoped, in spite of the information; but he answered with a placid countenance that he had never feared death, only that there was an intolerable burden upon his conscience.

That night was Cranmer's last. He began to learn by heart the words which he had prepared to utter on the morrow; then he broke off, saying that he would read them from the manuscript. He supped as usual, talked with companions till a late hour, went to bed and slept peacefully till five. Then he rose and prayed, and was shriven once more. Cole came to visit him again that morning, and asked if he had any money to give to the poor,—as condemned men usually did. He had none; and Cole bestowed upon him fifteen crowns for the purpose. Those about him were ill-pleased when, in giving a piece of silver to a poor old woman, he remarked that he would rather have the prayers of a good layman than those of a bad priest. Yet he was still arranging for funeral masses in the Colleges, and is said to have signed fourteen more copies of his recantation that morning. It was observed with some anxiety that a ring and a message were brought to him from a sister who had stuck to her Reformation principles; and they may indeed ha,ve had an effect upon the sensitive man. But he seemed not to falter. " Never fear," he is reported to have said to his friend the gaoler, as he thanked him and went out towards his execution ; " it was God who bent my mind and opinion at the beginning : I trust that He will complete the building which He has begun."

The morning of March 21 was foul and rainy. About nine o'clock, Lord Williams, with the Mayor and others, brought the prisoner out of Bocardo to be killed. Because of the wildness of the weather it had been decided that the sermon should not be preached at the stake as usual, but in St. Mary's Church. Cranmer carried in his bosom the paper upon which he had written out his last speech, in which he had purposed to profess publicly those Roman principles which he had now accepted. It is possible that he still hoped, even when he left Bocardo, that the profession would win him a reprieve. A friar walked on either side of him; and at the entrance of the Church they significantly began the Nunc Dimittis. If he had entertained any doubts before, the Song of Simeon must have certified him that his departure was at hand. They led him to a stage over against the pulpit, where he stood aloft that all the people might see him, " in a bare and ragged gown, and ill-favouredly clothed, with an old square cap " upon his head. In this habit, he " stood a good space upon the stage," waiting for the arrival of the preacher; and then, " turning to a pillar near adjoining thereunto, he lifted up his hands to heaven, and prayed unto God once or twice." While Cole's sermon was in progress, Cranmer was seen to be deeply moved. It was not the preacher's eloquence that moved him; it was the working of that inspiration which now came down upon him in answer to his prayer. He was determining to recant his recantation. " I shall not need," says an eyewitness, who took the side opposed to him, " for the time of sermon, to describe his behaviour, his sorrowful countenance, his heavy cheer, his face bedewed with tears; some time lifting

his eyes to heaven in hope, some time casting them doAvn to the earth for shame; to be brief, an image of sorrow, the dolour of his heart bursting out at his eyes in plenty of tears, retaining ever a quiet and grave behaviour, which increased the pity in men's hearts [so] that they unfeignedly loved him, hoping it had been his repentance for his transgression and error." And so indeed it was.

Sermon ended, the people began to hasten to the stake; but Cole called upon them to remain and hear the condemned man's profession of repentance and of faith, and to join in prayer for him. " I think," says the eyewitness, " there never was such a number so earnestly praying together. Love and hope increased devotion on every side." Then the Archbishop arose, put off his cap, drew forth from his bosom the paper which he had written, and said—" Good people, I had intended to desire you to pray for me, which because Mr. Doctor hath desired, and you have done already, I thank you most heartily for it. And now will I pray for myself, as I could best devise for mine own comfort, and say the prayer word for word as I have here written it." He added that there was one thing which grieved his conscience more than all the rest, of which he would speak by and by. Still standing upon his stage, he read aloud the beginning of his own Litany, and then went on with a pathetic entreaty. " Thou didst not give Thy Son unto death," he read, " 0 God the Father, for our little and small sins only, but for all the greatest sins of the world, so that the sinner returns unto Thee with a penitent heart, as I do here at this present." Then falling upon his knees and all the people along with him, he said the Lord's Prayer in

English, but it was observed that he added no Ave Maria. After that he stood up, and read his speech. He exhorted the people not to set overmuch by this glozing world, willingly and gladly to obey the King and Queen, to love one another with brotherly affection, to make a right use of riches—those who had them, He had been a long time in prison, he said, but he had heard of the great penury of the poor, and knew how dear victuals were at the time in Oxford. And now, he said—still reading—forsomuch as he was come to the last end of his life, and saw before his eyes heaven ready to receive him, or hell ready to swallow him up, he would declare to them his very faith, without colour or dissimulation, whatsoever he had written in times past. He rehearsed the Apostles' Creed. He said that he believed every article of the Catholic Faith, every word and sentence taught by our Saviour Jesus Christ, His Apostles and Prophets in the New and Old Testament, and all articles explicate and set forth in the General Councils.

" And now," he said—and he was still reading from the manuscript—" I come to the great thing that so troubleth my conscience more than anything that ever I did or said in my life; and that is the setting abroad"—but there Cranmer left his manuscript. In his manuscript he had written that the thing which troubled him was " the setting abroad untrue books and writings contrary to the truth of God's Word—the books which I wrote against the Sacrament of the Altar sith the death of King Henry VIII." What he said was, " the setting abroad of writings contrary to the truth; which now here I renounce and refuse, as things written with my hand contrary to the truth which I thought in my heart, and writ for fear of death and to save my life, if it might be; and that is, all such bills which I have written or signed with mine own hand since my degradation; 1 wherein I have written many things untrue. And forasmuch as my hand offended in writing contrary to my heart, therefore my hand shall first be punished. For if I may come to the fire, it shall be first burned. And as for the Pope, I refuse him, as Christ's enemy and antichrist, with all his false doctrine."

It was a strangely dramatic ending for one who usually cared so little for effect. The downright character of the man sets off the splendour of his action. God had allowed him to fall, that the miracle of his recovery might the more powerfully affect the Church for ever. As soon as his words were finished, he turned as white as ashes, and all trace of tears passed from his countenance. Lord Williams was the first to speak. " Are you in your senses ? " he cried, " do you know what you are doing ? " " That I do," said Cranmer. " You shall never clear yourself of those errors," cried Williams, " with that dissembling hand." " Alas, my lord," replied the Archbishop, " I have been a man that all my life loved plainness, and never dissembled till now against the truth, which I am most sorry for." He added that, for the sacrament, he believed as he had taught in his book against Gardiner. After that he was suffered to speak no more.

Amidst the hubbub of voices, some asking what had happened, some explaining and commenting angrily or exultingly, according to their predilections, Cranmer

1 It will be observed that this does not include his first two Submissions.

was hurried away to the place where Latimer and Ridley had been burned before him. So quick was the martyr's step that others could scarcely keep pace with him. The baulked friars ran beside him, endeavouring even yet to bring him round again. " Recollect yourself," urged John de Garcia, " do not die so desperately." " Away," Cranmer replied, " this fellow would have me take the Pope for head of the Church, when he is its tyrant." But his next answer was more like his habitual lowliness. "Assuredly," cried the friar,"you would have acknowledged him for head if he had spared your head." Cranmer felt that the thing was true. It was the murderous cruelty shown towards him which had brought him to his senses. There was a pause; and then the simple-hearted Archbishop answered—" Yes ; if he had saved me alive, I should have obeyed his laws." De Garcia reminded him that he had made his confession that morning. " Well," answered the Archbishop, purposely ignoring the point of the remark, " and is not confession a good thing ? "

" Coming to the stake with a cheerful countenance and willing mind," says the Papist eyewitness, " he put off his garments with haste, and stood upright in his shirt." The friars spoke to him no more; they said the devil was with him. When an Oxford divine, called Ely, began a disputation, Lord Williams cried—" Make short, make short." An iron chain fastened Cranmer to the stake. He appears to have taken from his bosom a signed copy of his Recantation, intending to throw it into the flames. Lord Williams plucked it from him. He offered his hand to some of the bystanders. To a last appeal from Ely, who chode those who accepted the sign of kindness, " the Bishop answered, showing his hand, 'This is the hand that wrote it, and therefore shall it suffer first punishment/ " 1

" Fire being now put to him," says the anonymous spectator, " he stretched out his right hand and thrust it into the flame, and held it there a good space, before the fire came to any other part of his body, where his hand was seen of every man sensibly burning, crying with a loud voice—' This hand hath offended.' " Only once he withdrew it from the fire to wipe his face. 2 f< As soon as the fire got up he was very soon dead, never stirring or crying all the while. His patience in the torment," continues the Papist, " his courage in dying, if it had been taken either for the glory of God, the wealth of his country, or the testimony of truth, I could worthily have commended the example, and matched it with the fame of any Father of ancient time." 3

So ended that great and troubled career. Men will

1 I am inclined to think that the quotation of St. Stephen's words, " I see heaven opened," which Bishop Cranmer's Re-cantacyons puts in his mouth, is a malicious reminiscence of what Cranmer had said in his speech in St. Mary's about heaven or hell being ready for him.

2 Foxe.

3 This account of Cranmer's end is for the most part taken from the letter of the anonymous Papist " J.A.," which is preserved among Foxe's MSS. in the British Museum (Harleian, 422, 10). It is printed by Strype, and reprinted by Todd, ii. 493 foil., though Mr. Dixon points out (iv. 532, note) that Strype has fused it with another document, containing Cranmer's "speech. I have added many details, however, from Bishop Crannt>r'::; Recantacyons—especially the dialogue on the way to the stake. With regard to this latter pamphlet, I am disposed to think, in spite of the contrary opinion of Mr. Gairdner, the editor, that it was written by Nicholas Harpslield. See the account of it in Dixon iv. 490.

continue to judge him very variously, according as they agree with his opinions or disagree; but it may be hoped that from henceforth one fault will not be so frequently laid to his charge—a fault which was wholly foreign to his character. Whatever else he was, Cranmer was no crafty dissembler. He was as artless as a child. Even those actions of his which have brought upon him the accusation of double dealing—the reservation with which he took the oath at his consecration, the acknowledgment that he should not have withdrawn his recantation if he had been allowed to live—are instances of his naive simplicity. He may sometimes have deceived himself; he never had any intention to deceive another. Trustful towards others, even to a fault, he had little confidence in himself. His humility amounted almost to a vice. His judgment was too easily swayed by those who surrounded him—especially by those in authority. In this way he frequently did or consented to things imposed upon him by others, which he would never have thought of by himself. He sheltered himself under the notion that he was a subordinate, when by virtue of his position he was necessarily a principal, and was surprised, and sometimes even irritated, that others did not see things in the same light. What was clear to himself he expected to be clear to others—even if the view was one to which he had himself but lately come. When others failed to assent to his opinions, he was inclined to reprove them somewhat too plainly for their ignorance and stupidity. The few men whom he had learned thoroughly to suspect, like Bishop Gardiner, he pursued relentlessly. Yet the least sign of a change would have made him relent. He was the most placable of men. " My Lord," said Heath, afterwards Queen Mary's Chancellor, " I now know how to win all things at your hands well enough." " How so ? " said Cranmer. " Mary," Heath replied, " I perceive that I must first attempt to do unto you some notable displeasure, and then by a little relenting obtain of you what I can desire." " Whereat my Lord bit his lip," says Morice, " as his manner was when he was moved, and said—' You say well, but yet you may be deceived.' " " He was a man of such temperature of nature, or rather so mortified," says his secretary, " that no manner of prosperity or adversity could alter or change his accustomed conditions. To the face of the world, his countenance, diet, or sleep commonly never altered." 1 He was indefatigable in his industry. His placid character knew no ambition. In an age of rapine, the friend of Henry remained unenriched. So courteous and amiable in his manners that his enemies found fault with him on that account, he was unstinting in his hospitality, especially towards scholars, and lavish in his gifts. Unless marriage is a sin, no breath ever assailed the purity of his life. He lived in constant prayer and penitence.

, Even those who cannot approve of all Cranrner's acts and opinions may well be thankful to the Divine Providence which at that crisis of history set him in his great place. A man of a more rigid mind would have snapped under the strain which he endured, and the continuity of the Church of England would have been greatly imperilled. If Gardiner, or Heath, or even Thirlby—to name some of the most statesmanlike of his contemporaries—had been put in the chair of St. Augustine when Cranmer was, they could not have 1 Morice pp. 245, 244.

maintained the position under Edward; and the place, if filled at all, would have been filled by some reckless innovator after the Swiss pattern. Cranmer's large mind and temper, while essentially conservative, was capable of taking in the new and of going great lengths with it, and yet of coordinating it with the old, instead of substituting the one for the other. In this way he was able to preserve, by means of the Prayerbook, the Ordinal, and the Articles, a truly Catholic footing for the Church of England. If, instead of an ever narrowing sect of adherents to the Papacy, confronted by a Protestantism which drifts farther and further away from the faith of the ancient Fathers, our country possesses a Church of unbroken lineage, true to the agelong inheritance in its framework of government, doctrine, and worship, yet open to every form of progress, and comprehensive enough to embrace every human being who confesses Christ, the thanks are due, under God, to the sagacity, the courage, the suppleness combined with firmness, of Archbishop Cranmer. The unparalleled splendour of his dying actions secured for ever to the Church of England what his life had gained. For two things Cranmer lived. He lived to restore, as nearly as might be, the Church of the Fathers; and he lived, and he died, for the rights and the welfare of England. The independence of the English Crown, the freedom of the English Church from an intolerable foreign yoke, an English Bible, the English services— for these he laboured with untiring and unostentatious diligence, and with few mistakes, considering the difficulties of his task. He made no claim to infallibility; but he laid open the way to the correction of whatever might be amiss in his own teaching or in

the Church which he ruled, when, in the magnificent demurrer which he made at his degradation, he appealed, not for himself only but for all those who should afterwards be on his side, to the next General Council. Under that broad shield which he threw over us, we may confidently abide, and lay our cause before those who will candidly weigh the facts of history.

THE END

Printed in Great Britain
by Amazon